"Stop laughing at my expense, or I'll..."
His eyes glittered with amusement.
"You'll do what?"
"...kiss you."

Rand's laughter died abruptly. He stared at Chelsea. His gaze, not the least amused, drifted to her lips. "Don't make threats you aren't prepared to carry out," he said softly.

Her heart was hammering very fast because underneath the cool polish of his reserve, Chelsea had the feeling he really did feel threatened. "Don't worry. I wouldn't kiss you right now anyway," she said breezily.

"Let's get something straight," he said. "You're not kissing me, ever."

She turned back and looked at him narrowly. So, he was still in his bossy, military mode, was he? "'Ever' is a long, long time, Mr. Peabody," she said huskily.

"Don't play with fire, Miss King."

But she could tell by the red-hot feeling tingling through her that she already was.

Dear Reader,

July might be a month for kicking back and spending time with family at outdoor barbecues, beach cottages and family reunions. But it's an especially busy month for the romance industry as we prepare for our annual conference. This is a time in which the romance authors gather to hone their skills at workshops, share their experiences and recognize the year's best books. Of course, to me, this month's selection in Silhouette Romance represents some of the best elements of the genre.

Cara Colter concludes her poignant A FATHER'S WISH trilogy this month with *Priceless Gifts* (#1822). Accustomed to people loving her for her beauty and wealth, the young heiress is caught off guard when her dutiful bodyguard sees beyond her facade…and gives *her* a most precious gift. Judy Christenberry never disappoints, and *The Bride's Best Man* (#1823) will delight loyal readers as a pretend dating scheme goes deliciously awry. Susan Meier continues THE CUPID CAMPAIGN with *One Man and a Baby*, (#1824) in which adversaries unite to raise a motherless child. Finally, Holly Jacobs concludes the month with *Here with Me* (#1825). A heroine who thought she craved the quiet life finds her life invaded by her suddenly meddlesome parents and a man she's never forgotten and his adorable toddler.

Be sure to return next month when Susan Meier concludes her CUPID CAMPAIGN trilogy and reader-favorite Patricia Thayer returns to the line to launch the exciting new BRIDES OF BELLA LUCIA miniseries.

Happy reading!

Ann Leslie Tuttle
Associate Senior Editor

Please address questions and book requests to:
Silhouette Reader Service
U.S.: 3010 Walden Ave., P.O. Box 1325, Buffalo, NY 14269
Canadian: P.O. Box 609, Fort Erie, Ont. L2A 5X3

Priceless Gifts

CARA COLTER

A Father's Wish

SILHOUETTE **Romance**®

Published by Silhouette Books

America's Publisher of Contemporary Romance

With gratitude to everyone at my
Silhouette Romance family for making the
past eighteen years a journey of pure Light.

 **SILHOUETTE BOOKS**

ISBN-13: 978-0-373-19822-1
ISBN-10:   0-373-19822-1

PRICELESS GIFTS

Visit Silhouette Books at www.eHarlequin.com

Printed in U.S.A.

CARA COLTER

shares ten acres in the wild Kootenay region of British Columbia with the man of her dreams, three children, two horses, a cat with no tail and a golden retriever who answers best to "bad dog." She loves reading, writing and the woods in winter (no bears). She says life's delights include an automatic garage door opener and the skylight over the bed that allows her to see the stars at night. She also says, "I have not lived a neat and tidy life, and used to envy those who did. Now I see my struggles as having given me a deep appreciation of life, and of love, that I hope I succeed in passing on through the stories that I tell."

Cast of Characters for *A Father's Wish*

Brandgwen "Brandy" King—The brave King "princess." This tomboy found the greatest adventure of all with her new husband and his baby daughter.

Jessica "Jessie" King—The brainy King "princess." She discovered the passion within her own heart when she fell for her father's archrival.

Chelsea King—The beautiful King "princess." Will she learn that there is more to life—and to *herself*—than what's on the surface?

Jacob King—A magnate whose dying wish is to see his three daughters happily in love, even if that means doing some heavy-handed matchmaking!

Prologue

Jacob King stared at the letter in his hand. The paper rattled and he realized he was trembling. It was obscene that one sheet of paper, so cheap that it was nearly transparent, could cause such mingled fear and fury. He set the letter down, pinched the bridge of his nose and then looked at his head of security, Cameron McPherson.

Wasn't this the way of life? Just when you thought everything was going your way, that you had been blessed beyond your wildest dreams, in came the curveball. Or, in this case, the time bomb. Who controlled it? When was it set to go off? Was it real or a dud?

"How many of these has she received?" he asked Cameron.

"A dozen so far, each one more aggressive than the last. This one particularly concerns us because it sounds like the perp has been in her house and knows her daily routines."

Perp, Jake thought sickly. He didn't want a word like that used in reference to any part of his life, and certainly not in reference to his precious youngest daughter, his baby, Chelsea.

At twenty-two, Chelsea would resent being called a baby, and yet Jake had never felt more protective of her than he did right now. "Is she safe?"

There was a fraction of a second's hesitation before Cameron said, "Yes."

"But?"

"Her lifestyle is very high profile. She's too public. We have to damp her down until we get to the bottom of this."

Easier said than done when it came to Chelsea.

"One of the maids here at Kingsway told me a man had approached her and offered her one hundred dollars for Chelsea's toothbrush or hairbrush."

Jake shuddered at the creepiness of it. "Related to these letters?" he asked.

"We don't know yet," Cameron admitted. "I've been handling her security, personally, since the arrival of the sixth letter, but I'm hoping to hand her over to someone else."

"Why?"

Cameron looked uncomfortable. "The family connection is making it awkward."

Cameron's brother, Clint, was married to Chelsea's sister, Jake's oldest daughter, Brandy. Trust Chelsea to somehow make that into a difficult situation for Cameron.

"Is that a diplomatic way of saying my daughter is

being headstrong and rebellious and not amenable to your suggestions, Cameron?"

Cameron grinned, ducked his head, then became all business again. "The man I have in mind is on leave from, um, a government assignment. He's brilliant, highly trained and tough."

"More than a match for my daughter," Jake said dryly.

"The problem is that this isn't his normal type of assignment."

A diplomatic way to say the man didn't want the job, Jake assumed. "Offer him whatever it takes."

"It's not about money."

Jake sighed. That kind of person was such a rarity he might be tempted to think one did not really exist, if his son-in-law, husband to his middle daughter, Jessie, had not just recently proven him so wrong.

Only moments ago Jake had been reliving his matchmaking victories and plotting his final effort. He was eighty-three years old and dying. His only wish was for happiness for the three daughters born to him so late in his life. He'd been so delightfully good at meddling with Brandgwen's and Jessica's lives that he was actually going to miss the activity once he succeeded in finding love for Chelsea. But finding a suitable match for his youngest daughter was proving a more difficult task than he'd anticipated. Though Chelsea possessed a rare beauty that could stop a conversation, she had chosen to move in a world that required very little of her. It seemed to be all about the looks, the clothes, the parties.

How could Jake hope to find a man for her—someone who would see beyond her headlong pursuit

of the silly and the superficial to the beauty of her soul—
when she seemed so determined not to see that herself?
It suddenly seemed achingly trite that he had wished to
find her love—the only true beauty—before he died.
Now, every goal but keeping her safe seemed small and
insignificant.

Maybe it was surprising that Chelsea had not been
stalked before. Jake could read in the morning paper
what she had for breakfast or what kind of shoes she
bought on a shopping spree.

People were overly fascinated with her and her lifestyle. But he was assuming the perp was a stranger.

"I wonder if it's Sarah," Jake mumbled, and then re-
gretted even thinking of it. "Never mind." Of course it
couldn't be Sarah.

But then what did he really know of Sarah Jane
McKenzie? He would have bet his life that his sweet
assistant would never have stolen from anyone, let
alone from him. She'd disappeared before Jake had a
chance to ask her the question that burned in his heart.
Why?

Had Sarah envied Chelsea, who had been nothing but
kind to her? Envied her enough to threaten her?

"It's not Sarah," Cameron said.

Jake looked up, surprised at the testiness in the man's
voice. Ah, yes, Sarah had broken more than just Jake's
heart with her betrayal of trust.

"We want to tuck Chelsea away somewhere, somewhere no one would think to look for her," Cameron said,
moving on hurriedly from the touchy subject of Sarah.

Jake nodded. Thanks to Jessica and Garner he had
just rediscovered such a sanctuary, renewed connec-

tions with long-lost family members. Before their wedding he had been fifty years removed from the Virginia mountains where he had come to maturity. He was certain no one would ever look for his fast lane daughter there.

Chelsea, naturally, would hate it.

"Come in," he called, when there a was a firm knock on the door.

A man came into Jake's office, power in every line of his face, his body, his carriage.

Raven haired, his jade eyes swept the room before coming to rest on Jake. He would have been exceedingly handsome once, but one side of his face was scarred now.

Cameron said, with obvious relief, "Rand. Randall Peabody, Jacob King."

Rand crossed the room, all grace, leashed power and alertness, tigerlike. His grip was like steel; his gaze made Jake feel stripped to his soul.

"Rand is the man I asked to consider taking on Chelsea. Until we get to the bottom of this. Rand, I assume since you're here…"

Rand glanced at Cameron, gave him a slight nod.

Jake eyed the man, and then allowed himself to savor the sense of relief that washed over him. If anyone could keep his headstrong daughter safe from harm it was the man in front of him. Rand radiated an iron will, fearsome strength, confidence in his ability to control things lesser men might back away from. Which summed up Chelsea to a T.

For the first time since Jake had looked at that misspelled, trashy letter that had promised a terrible fate for his daughter, he relaxed. "Thank you," Jake said softly, and he saw a flicker of compassion in the flinty depths. Chelsea would be safe. He studied Rand again, and actually felt a smile tug at his lips. Unhappy, no doubt, but safe.

Chapter One

Rand Peabody decided he was in hell. And he was a man, after all, who knew a thing or two about hell.

Or had deluded himself into thinking he did.

Unobtrusively, keeping one hand steady on the wheel of the sleek silver car he drove, keeping his eyes straight ahead, Rand reached up and touched the ridged scars that ran from his temple to his jaw line, the entire length of the left side of his face.

Oh, yeah, he'd thought he knew about hell.

Until now.

Because now he was seated in a car that for all its luxury and size seemed way, way too small, and the young woman in the passenger seat could easily be the most beautiful in the world.

Her hair was a shade of silver-blond Rand had never seen before, and it fell in a cascading wave over her slender, golden shoulders. Despite the day and age he lived in, he was pretty sure the unearthly color of both her hair and her skin was completely natural.

The word hazel did not do justice to her eyes, which were an astonishing blend of colors shot through with threads of golds and greens and deep browns. Her bone structure was something artists tried to capture, a perfect symphony of lines, exquisite high cheekbones, delicate nose, a surprisingly strong jaw, her lips full, red and pouty. Only her posture belied the sophistication of the rest of her image. Her figure was reed slender, a hint of her youth and vulnerability in the faint hunch of her shoulders, the slender arms crossed protectively over her breasts.

She wore the uniform of young women her age—low slung jeans, a wide belt, a narrow strapped white tank top. But she wore them differently than most, or maybe pure expense bought that exquisite fit that said *rich*. If the fit hadn't said it, the abundant tangle of gold chains that winked against her neck and trailed down to the cleft between her breasts certainly would have.

The scent that wafted off of her was delicate and faintly sweet, like a silk scarf that had brushed lightly against jasmine. The scent suggested a certain pliable femininity that was at odds with her expression— haughty, mutinous, angry.

He'd seen pictures of Chelsea King, of course. You could not live in the world and not have seen her. The face of the youngest of Jake King's *princesses* sold magazines. The public had an insatiable desire to know the smallest details about her: Her hairstyles, her clothes, her pets, her antics, her friends, even her occasional forays into a normal grocery store were all treated as newsworthy, as if she was as important and as interesting as peace talks in the Middle East, cancer cures, or the president.

She probably got a lot more press than the president. And sitting beside her now, Rand understood why. The pictures had not done her any kind of justice. Her beauty, her actual presence, was almost drugging in its potency and power.

Which put him in a strange kind of hell. He was sworn to protect her—being caught off guard by her sheer magnetism made him aggravated with himself.

Thankfully he knew himself to be a disciplined man.

And also thankfully, though it annoyed him, this exquisitely beautiful woman did not seem to know he existed. A robot drove her car, someone so far beneath her that he was invisible. Would she have felt that way before an explosion had claimed part of his face?

That was the kind of question he did not ask himself, ever.

She had just terminated one cell phone call when her phone rang again. The ring tone was discordant, something he recognized vaguely as hip-hop, a sound he hated already.

He braced himself for what would follow the sound.

Right on cue, she spoke, her husky voice filled with all the drama and angst young women of her age seemed to muster over absolutely nothing.

"Oh, my God, Lindsay, my father has lost his mind."

You're not going to believe this, he guessed silently and cynically.

"You're not going to believe this…."

And then the rest of the whole sorry story. Her father's plan, her refusal, Jake King pulling out the big guns: goodbye allowance, credit cards and car.

Can you believe this is my life? he guessed.

"Can you believe this is my life? I'm a prisoner!"

He knew a thing or two about being a prisoner. It had been part of his personal tour of hell. But there was really no point trying to educate her, or involving himself personally with her in any way.

Her idea of being a prisoner meant life was unfair. She was being spirited away to the ends of the earth against her will, and where she was going she didn't think there would be a decent latte. She was going to miss the wrap party for Barry's movie when she'd already chosen a spectacular Marchesa dress.

Rand didn't know who Barry was, or Lindsay, or Marchesa, either, though when he got around to reading the thick manila folder he'd been provided with, he was sure he'd find out.

Since Rand had now heard her litany of complaints at least half a dozen times, he focused on the road. Had she been waiting for his attention to drift a tiny bit? Was she more aware of his presence than she'd let on? Because a tiny change to her voice alerted him he'd better listen.

"Virginia," she whispered.

He felt her shoot a little look his way. That's all he had asked of her. Don't tell anyone where she was headed. A precaution, he'd said blandly, for now.

He should have known precautions wouldn't interest her. She didn't know the full story; Jake's decision, which Rand had not been in agreement with. She was an adult. Let her know what was going on. Tell her about the letters, show her a few of them. The content should manage to put the fear of God into Miss Chelsea King. But he'd been vetoed, and that was that. Putting fear into her rarified world, even justified fear, was not something her well meaning but overly protective father was allowing.

Rand made a decision, not based entirely on the fact that if she kept talking the whole world would soon know she was at her aunt's farm in Virginia. After a full—he glanced at his watch—forty-two minutes in the car with her, he was fed up with the whining. Didn't she know there were people in the world with real problems?

Without even glancing at her, giving no warning what was coming, he reached over—all that military training would be useful on this ridiculous assignment after all—snatched her cell phone from her and, in one smooth move, had his window down and the phone on the highway behind them. It disappeared under the front tire of a semi-truck and trailer.

There was a moment's blessed silence. For the first time since he'd been introduced to her, he had Miss King's full attention.

"You can't do that!" she sputtered.

He didn't say anything, since it was more than obvious he already had.

"Oh, my God," she said, her amazing eyes sparking with fury. "You can't do that!"

He shrugged, focused on the road, but very aware that her fists were curling and uncurling impotently. Was it possible the little princess was going to take a swing at him?

The thought was downright funny.

He tried to remember the last time he had found anything really amusing, and didn't think it spoke very well of his life that he came up empty.

Disappointingly she gained control of herself and wrestled with her rebellious hands. In a tone as cold as ice she informed him, "I am going to have you fired."

He steeled himself not to react, though the amusement buzzed in him, annoyingly hard to swat down, like a mosquito after you'd gone to bed.

When he didn't give her a reaction, she added. "Immediately."

"Difficult to do with no phone," he said, biting the inside of his cheek, hard. "The immediately part, anyway."

She looked at him suspiciously, as if she had detected his amusement. He squinted harder at the road.

"I don't know who you think you are, but you can't behave that way to me." Her voice quivered with outrage.

"Rand Peabody," he said, keeping his voice deliberately dry. They'd been introduced, but she had been so busy supervising the loading of her bags into the trunk of the car that she hadn't taken a bit of notice. Keeping one hand on the steering wheel he extended the other.

She glared at him and then at his hand and then tossed her mane of shimmering hair.

"I can't believe this is my life," she snapped. She did not take his hand, and in some small way that he understood completely, he was glad.

At least they had found common ground. Rand understood what it felt like to have your life spin out of control.

"That cell phone," she informed him, "had top secret numbers in it."

To himself he said, *Lady, don't kid yourself that you have any idea what top secret means.*

But outwardly he said nothing, which she took as an invitation to keep talking.

"I have the phone numbers of some of the most famous people in the world." She began to name the names that appeared with regularity in the celebrity rags. *Lindsay. Barry. Ashley. Paris. Orlando.*

"I think those last two were places, not people," he offered, deadpan.

"That shows what you know! These people are important."

"Nobel short listers for sure." He allowed just the faintest trace of sarcasm into his voice.

She sighed heavily and when she spoke it was in a princess-to-peasant tone. "If that phone falls into the wrong hands, I'll have a lot of people really, really angry with me. You could be sued."

There was the laughter again, pressing at his throat, wanting out *badly*.

He managed to choke out a noncommittal *ummhmm*.

She looked daggers at him. "I *need* that phone."

He knew, firsthand, what human beings *needed*. Food, water, shelter. Everything else, *everything*, was icing.

"You don't have to worry about the phone. It's not falling into anybody's hands. A semi ran over it."

Her mouth moved indignantly. "A truck ran over *my* phone?"

He nodded.

"Are you sure?"

He nodded again.

"Oh! What am I supposed to do without my phone numbers in the godforsaken wilderness?"

"Take up yoga?" he suggested mildly.

Her eyes narrowed on his face. "Are you suggesting something?"

That she was wound way too tight and she was far too caught up in a superficial world? That she could probably use a few days without a phone growing out of her ear? That she had no idea what the real world was all about and maybe it was time she learned?

Not his place to say so. "No, ma'am," he said.

"Don't call me ma'am. Ugh. It makes me feel old."

"Yes, ma'am." *Don't tell me what to do. It makes me feel mean.*

Her mouth moved silently, while she debated whether to argue with him. Then her whole tone changed.

"Why would you do that?" she asked plaintively. "Just toss my phone out the window?"

"Poor impulse control," he conceded.

"I am having you fired. As soon as I can."

"Okay."

"That wouldn't upset you?" She was obviously very disappointed by that.

"Good God, no."

She paused, glared at him. "So, you didn't want this job?" She said that with utter disbelief as if it was incomprehensible to her that someone in the world wouldn't be delighted to hang out in her shadow.

"Not particularly." Baby-sitting duty for some spoiled rotten rich kid was not exactly an elite assignment for a man who had lived most of his adult life as a warrior, on the very cutting edge of danger.

"And you're going to take that out on me?"

"Not if you get me fired," he reminded her mildly. Unfortunately he already knew what her chances of succeeding at that were.

Nil.

Because he knew something she didn't know.

She'd been receiving hate mail. A lot of it. It was mail she had never seen, in her protected little world of lattes and wrap parties and dress fittings. She wasn't going to her aunt's farm on a whim of her father's. And Rand wasn't making her keep the location secret from her friends to torment her. Chelsea King was going there for her own protection. Whoever was writing those letters knew way too much about the youngest heiress to the Auto Kingdom fortune.

But what no one seemed to know about was Jake's family connections in Virginia. His second daughter's marriage there, just a short time ago, had been kept entirely out of the press. Hetta King's farm, according to Jake, was remote enough that no one unfamiliar with the area would ever find it without explicit directions. And the town was small enough that if a stranger showed up and started asking questions, Hetta would be sure to hear about it.

To Rand, the situation was not ideal, but he rarely found any situation ideal. It would pose even greater challenges to try to hole up elsewhere with the very recognizable and extremely social Miss King.

The last letter had made it apparent that the perp had been inside her house without her knowledge—and without tripping up a very sophisticated security system. Was it someone in her inner circle who had turned against her? If so, she should still be safe in Virginia.

No one in that inner circle knew about Hetta. Chelsea herself had needed a moment to remember the older woman when her father told her she was going to see her aunt Hetta.

Rand probably would have had to relieve her of the cell phone at some point, anyway, to control who she talked to and when, at least until he had a better idea of who could be trusted and who couldn't.

"I really don't like you," she decided snootily.

When he didn't respond, she added, "A lot."

He still said nothing, kept his face like a stone, looking straight ahead.

But the truth was that again, for the sixth time in just as many minutes, Rand Peabody actually felt like laughing. And the last time he had felt that way had been so long ago he had begun to think laughter was frozen inside of him, a distant winter that could not remember the warmth of summer.

Chelsea King wanted to scream. Nobody had prepared her for Randall J. Peabody. In fact nothing in her existence had prepared her for Randall J. Peabody!

The name had implied an absolute lie: that her new bodyguard would be the same as her former one—old, faintly paternal, easily delegated to the background. She had not expected a man who was forceful, formidable and not the least intimidated by her status and even less interested in her wishes.

And that didn't begin to say anything about his *presence*.

The man was drop-dead gorgeous in a way that was different from the glamorous people she hung out with, the beautiful people that the paparazzi chased from party to premiere to afternoon tea. Rand Peabody was extraordinarily handsome in a way that was faintly weathered, world-weary, *real*. His teeth had not been whitened, his tan had not come from a booth. Even the scars that ran the length of the left side of his face added something to his raw appeal, rather than detracting from it. He radiated a rugged assurance in his own power, and, for some reason, his pure, unconscious confidence had made her feel young and foolish from the moment she had first seen him.

The cut of his thick black hair was short, not quite military, but hinting that it might have been that short not so long ago. His facial features were clean and hard. Implacable strength was stamped into them and into the stern set of his mouth and jaw.

He was big, she guessed him to be over six feet, and the body beneath the perfect fit of an expensive navy-blue suit looked chiseled—and not the kind of chiseled that came from the gym, either. Though Rand looked to be thirty or so—not that much older than her own twenty-two years—there was a look in his eyes, deep and startlingly green, that made her shiver. He had seen things that were not part of her world.

From the moment he had stepped forward, from that group of men gathered in her father's office, she had been fighting not to let Randall J. Peabody know she was acutely, horribly aware of him and his intense masculinity in a way that rattled her world.

As if her world was not rattled enough!

How could this be her life? How could things unravel so quickly? With absolutely no warning?

One minute she'd been chatting on the phone with Jennifer, talking about the dresses they were being offered by various designers, and the next she'd been on the carpet in her father's office. At first he'd been so sweet—the daddy she always knew. But his request! That she go help the aging aunt she'd only met once on a farm in Farewell, Virginia.

Chelsea was pretty sure she didn't like farms. But she was really sure she didn't like new situations. She had been diagnosed with dyslexia when she was in the seventh grade. The problem had been left undiagnosed for so long because she had perfected rebellion as a defense. Better to seem angry, haughty or difficult than stupid! Even after the diagnosis, all her father's money and the extra help it had gotten for her had not made learning one iota easier. She still hated being in situations where she might be seen as not quick to catch on, *stupid*.

A farm definitely qualified as an unfamiliar situation. She didn't know what was expected of her. Better not to have to find out. She'd told her father she had commitments. Her calendar for the next six months was full, full, full.

"Daddy," she'd said sweetly, "if Aunt Betty—"

"Hetta," he corrected her, and she heard that first disconcerting hint of steel in his voice.

"—needs help on her farm, I'm sure we could hire someone for her." She saw the look of disappointment on his face and added quickly, "I could find someone."

Then her father had become someone she didn't know at all.

Just like that he'd suspended her allowance, canceled her credit cards and taken her car keys. Rand Peabody had put his hand over his mouth, but she knew he'd laughed at her, thoroughly enjoying her humiliation. It had been a lot of years since anyone had dared to mock her, and she didn't like it one little bit.

She'd been hustled into some terribly drab car, with this absolutely intimidating man, hardly time to pack the bags she needed.

She wasn't putting up with this!

She really didn't like Rand Peabody. Okay, he was gorgeous, but that said, there was something about him that was cold and distastefully domineering, and she'd thought that even before he'd laughed at her and disposed of her phone in such a barbaric manner.

She slid a look his way.

His expression was closed, uninviting. Gorgeous, too, especially on this side, his good side. The other side had a legacy of scars running the length of it that spoke of a dangerous life, dangerous places, dangerous choices. Why had her father entrusted her to a man who was so obviously familiar with a side of life from which she had been completely sheltered?

"We'll see about that," she muttered to herself. When her father heard about Mr. Peabody's behavior with the phone, that would be it for him. Her father wasn't going to let anybody throw her property around!

Was he?

She had the unsettling feeling she didn't know who her father was. He'd become so implacable about her visit to her aunt. Sheesh. Farewell, Virginia.

Her sister had just gotten married there less than a month ago. Though still in Europe, touring in old cars—what kind of honeymoon was that?—Jessie was actually going to live in Farewell someday. A place with no Starbucks!

Chelsea was pleased about her sister's happiness. She'd never seen Jessie so gloriously and deliriously in love. But both Chelsea's sisters' marriages, and her friend Sarah's betrayal, had happened in such quick and unexpected succession. To add to her sense of her world's instability, her father did not look well or seem to have his normal vigor. It all added up to Chelsea feeling shaken, wanting to cling to the world she knew, where her sisters loved her and her father would always be there for her.

The truth was, after Jessie's wedding, Chelsea hadn't been able to get out of Farewell fast enough. Sleepy would have been too exciting a description of the place. *Catatonic*, she decided, pleased with herself, since words were not her specialty.

She wanted the fast lane, glamor, parties, flashbulbs going off in her face, a world where being *smart* had nothing at all to do with recognition. The last thing she wanted to do was pause for breath or think about the events of the last few weeks and what they meant to her. She didn't want to *feel* the sneaky little fear that tried to catch her in unsuspecting moments: that life—her life— was changing whether she wanted it to or not; that she was not really sure who she could trust; that, when she had seen her sister Brandy with her husband Clint and then Jessie with Garner, Chelsea had felt an unbearable sense of loneliness, of her full life being strangely, inexplicably empty.

She glanced again at the man beside her.

His face was emotionless. He didn't care about her or her cell phone or the unexpected trials of her life.

Imagine anyone thinking of her, Chelsea King, as an unpleasant assignment.

Most people would love to have a chance to be with her, to glimpse her world. Last year she'd agreed to spend the day with someone who'd won a contest to be with her. A day with Chelsea King had been their wildest dream come true. She thought of telling Randall Peabody that, but another glance at his profile revealed she'd be wasting her breath.

He didn't even look her way. She wondered what it would take to move him, wondered how he would react if she changed tactics: touched his arm, asked him about himself.

She decided he would not be fooled, and she might end up being the one who felt foolish. She hung out with up and coming young actors in Hollywood. She had dated them and been at their parties. She had been sought after by rich, handsome young men whose families could claim greater wealth than her own. She had e-mailed chatty little notes and photos to a prince for a few memorable months last year. Though she was not an actress or a model, she had seen herself referred to as the "it" girl on many, many occasions. And yet, looking at Rand Peabody's hard profile, she was aware he was out of her league. She would do well not to try to play with him.

It would be the proverbial playing with fire.

She folded her arms across her chest and looked out the window, determined to look anywhere but at him. It was going to be a long and tedious trip. She didn't do well at tedium. Perhaps she'd get away from him at a rest stop. She entertained the delicious notion for a few minutes, but realized it fell into the same dangerous category as touching his arm. He would not be a man in the least entertained by childish displays of rebellion. If she was going to escape, she would need to succeed at the effort. It would require stealth and planning. *Planning.* Not exactly her forte.

Surprisingly, she was aware of becoming relaxed, of liking the scent of him, even as she fought her liking for it: masculine, real, a scent that reminded her of a moment in Switzerland with her father, long ago, when the mountain air had been crisp and good and pure. Then her eyes grew heavy, and she fell asleep.

Chelsea awoke when the car jolted to a stop. For a moment she felt foggy and disoriented. Then she realized she had not woken at all. Instead she was in the middle of a nightmare. For pressed against the other side of the very same car window her cheek was pressed against was a slathering monster.

She stared at the huge bald head, the ogre ears, the beady eyes and the pink, slimy snout, trying to comprehend, but comprehension didn't come. Instead the monster squealed and grunted hideously and butted against the glass leaving a trail of slime from his round, flat snout.

Chelsea screamed. When the beast bunted the glass again as if he was trying to get a better look at her—as if he might break through the window barrier—instinct took over. She scrambled over the gearshift and directly into Rand Peabody's lap.

He placed a finger to her lips, and she looked into the calm darkness of his astounding green eyes. She saw strength there and fearlessness. He said something to her, in a foreign tongue, the words musical and reassuring. Fear vanished, and she stared, mesmerized, astonished by the fact that she felt safe though a real monster butted the window again.

Chelsea buried her head against Rand's chest. Beneath her cheek, his chest rose and fell with the beat of his heart, strong and steady. His hand found her hair, and everything faded, save for him. It felt as if she would never have to fear monsters again.

Then the hand dropped from her hair and opened his car door. His hand circled her waist, and she was unceremoniously dropped off his lap. He slid out from under her and was out of the car. He glanced back at her.

"It's only a pig," he said, then shut the door, leaving her trapped by the monster.

Only a pig?

She watched as Rand went around to her side of the car and confronted the monster. The nasty beast had a rhinestone encrusted collar on its neck, as if it was someone's demented idea of a pet. Rand actually patted the pig on its grotesquely large head. She saw a vaguely familiar old lady come out of a tiny white house. She joined Rand and the pig.

Rand Peabody looked over at Chelsea, gestured for her to come out of the car, and actually threw back his head and laughed when she crossed her arms over her chest and shook her head in absolute refusal. His laughter changed everything—made him somehow boyish, approachable, charming—far more dangerous than he had been before.

She reminded herself, grimly, that the laughter was at her expense and not for the first time, either. She reminded herself how quickly he had put her off his lap. The pig nudged his hand looking for more affection, and Rand, who had been rather stingy with his affection toward her moments ago, scratched the greedy beast willingly. The pig leaned into his hand and moaned with an almost human sound of satisfaction.

Chelsea King, eyeing that gorgeous man, tried to decide if she had ever been more insulted in her life. Mr. Peabody appeared to be more receptive to being touched by a pig than by her!

Chapter Two

"What's wrong with her?"

The old woman peered past Rand to where Chelsea sat, her arms wrapped around herself looking gorgeous…and mutinous.

"She's scared of your pig," Rand said, and wondered why it was he could see straight through that haughty expression on Chelsea King's face.

"What kind of person is scared of a pig?" Hetta King asked disdainfully.

Rand marveled at his odd desire to defend Chelsea. He supposed there were all kinds of people who would be afraid of pigs. There was probably a fancy name for it, like people who were afraid to come out of their houses. *Swineophobes. Hographobics.* But he bit back his defense, partly because it unsettled him that he wanted to make it, and partly because of the look of frank adoration on the old woman's face as she studied her pig.

"Especially a pig like Benjamin Franklin," she said, then turned abruptly and shoved a work-hardened hand at him. "Hetta King," she said. "You must be Peabody, not quite what I was expecting with a name like that. Chelsea and I met briefly at Jessica's wedding. Snooty kid."

Again, he felt an odd defensiveness that he bit back.

"I wouldn't have been quite so accommodating about having her here if I'd known she was scared of pigs."

That's when he started to laugh. The situation was deliciously absurd. The laughter came slowly, like rusty water moving through a pipe that had not been used for a long time. Then it ran sweet and clear.

"Hmph," Hetta said, after he'd composed himself. She regarded him through squinting eyes. "What happened to your face?"

He'd always appreciated directness. "I was in an explosion."

"You were probably way too pretty before, anyway. I can't abide a pretty man. I know that look about you," she said. "I seen plenty of boys come home from wars. I don't know how the princess will handle it, but this place will do your soul good. Life's plain. Air is sweet. Food is good."

He was embarrassed that his damaged soul showed so easily, but still he looked around and knew her words were probably true. The farm stood in the shadow of the Appalachian mountains, green, thickly wooded, mysterious. It was a small piece of cultivation at the edge of a wilder place. The buildings were all neat and white-washed; the garden was fenced; bright flowers sprouted around the house. The air, when he drew it deep into his lungs, had a purity to it, crisp and clean as drinking from a mountain stream.

"Hey!"

He and Hetta looked over at the car. Chelsea had unrolled the window and was leaning out. "Remember me? The one you're being paid to protect?"

He wondered how she had gotten so good at pretending she was angry when she was afraid, and he wondered again, uneasily, how he knew that about her. One of his specialties, he reminded himself, was reading people. He was darned good at it, too. But somehow being able to tell the truth from a lie, or a dangerous person from a benign one, was far different from being able to read the sensitivities of a very complex woman.

Of course the mask of haughtiness had failed completely when Chelsea spotted poor Benjamin's snout pressed against her window, the scream had nearly ruptured Rand's eardrums. And then, before he'd had time to prepare himself, she'd practically climbed up him to get away from the pig. For an instant, he had felt a surging protectiveness, a *need*, male and primal, to take away her fears, to keep her from any harm. It was a need that went far deeper than what he was being paid for.

But that rather noble feeling had quickly been chased away by another need, also male and also primal, caused by the soft pliancy of her curves pressed into him. Despite her spoiled brat persona, Chelsea King was no little girl. No. She was one hundred percent lush, sensuous, *tempting* woman. He had not had a woman that close to him in nearly as long as he had not laughed. He had felt almost weak with the sudden desire to hold her harder. He had not been able to fight the impulse to touch the silvery strands of her hair. They had not disappointed. Her hair had run through the toughness of his hands like a healing balm, unbelievably soft, unimaginably silky. At the impulse to bury his nose in it, he had put her off of him as if his legs had caught fire. He was not a man who tolerated weakness well, not in others and certainly not in himself.

"Excuse me!" she called now, like she might call a chauffeur to get her bags. "Cooking in the car over here."

"So, get out of it." He wasn't going to be her slave, even if he did know she was afraid and trying very hard to hide it with that imperious tone. Sorry, not in his job description. Her aunt took one look at his expression and snickered happily.

Chelsea's tone of voice changed. "I can't get out. That pig might touch me. If he put his nose on my leg…" She shuddered.

He sighed, knowing he had to reward her honesty, even as he recognized his own vulnerability to it. He strolled over and yanked open the door. This was what he was paid to do, to protect her, even from pigs.

He bowed. "Princess."

She eyed the pig warily, then tucked herself close to his side, making sure to keep him between the pig and herself.

"The pig is tame," he said, gruffly.

"A tame pig is the most absurd thing I have ever heard." Her voice held a quiver that the judgment was intended to disguise but didn't.

"Well, you've led a sheltered life then."

"Oh, sure, just because I haven't been around pigs, tame or otherwise. Thank God for small mercies."

Despite how aggravating she was being, actually hiding behind him as her aunt and the pig came out to meet them, he felt the unexpected urge to laugh again. An urge that was killed when, immediately following introductions, she ordered him to unload her bags. Should he tell her he knew the more fragile she felt the more bratty she acted? No, no sense revealing how easily he read her. Instead Rand folded his arms over his chest, and Hetta, seeing the look on his face, called her pig and headed for the house.

"Benjamin Franklin," Chelsea said, giving her head a sad shake. "If he goes in that house, I'm not."

The pig followed Hetta right through the back door.

"Okay, never mind the bags. I'm not staying here."

He popped the trunk and started dumping her luggage on the ground.

"Did you hear me? I'm not staying here. The pig is in the house!"

"I heard you. Now you hear me. We're staying here. It is not open for discussion. And for your information, I am not your servant and I'm not going to be ordered around like some seventeenth century lackey. Got it?"

"Winslow always carried my bags," she said petulantly.

"Well, I'm not going to."

"It would be the gentlemanly thing to do." She blinked at him, all helpless female.

"I'm no gentleman."

She glared at him and the helpless female evaporated. "That is becoming increasingly obvious!"

"Good."

Without warning her expression changed, softened, which of course, was far more dangerous to him than her rich-girl haughtiness. He was beginning to suspect the *real* Chelsea King was not a bit like what she showed the world. But if her true nature remained a suspicion, that would be okay with him.

She lowered her voice. "What did that mean, what you said to me in the car?"

"What?" he was genuinely puzzled, guarded.

"You said something to me."

"You mean after you nearly broke my eardrums when Benjamin was getting a little friendly at the window?"

She nodded.

"I think I said don't be afraid."

"You said la *takhafii*, or something like that."

He was startled. He hadn't been aware that he had switched languages. Not being *aware* was a problem in his business. What exactly was this witch/child/woman doing to him?

"What language was that?" she pressed.

He hesitated. There was a whole part of his life he didn't discuss with anyone. It came out in his dreams. He awoke sometimes with the poetry of that language on his lips, but he was astonished he had spoken it to her. It would be a ridiculous slip in caution to think he could trust her, of all people, with that part of himself.

"What language was it?" she insisted.

"Arabic," he said, reluctantly. "It means don't be frightened."

"Arabic," she said surprised, her curiosity piqued. "Are you fluent in it?"

"I guess that would depend what you call fluent," he

said curtly. He didn't want Chelsea King getting personal with him, ferreting out information about his private life. It was going to be hard enough—as he knew from having her on his lap in the car—keeping this whole deal professional.

"I suppose if you're an educated man that would explain your sensitivity."

"Sensitivity?" he echoed. Now there was something he had not been accused of often! And certainly not by members of the opposite sex.

"You know. To being told what to do."

"Oh." *That* sensitivity.

"Why on earth are you doing this job? I mean it's obvious you are very worldly and educated."

Oh, he was educated all right. She just wouldn't want to know where he'd gotten that education and at what price.

"Good question," he said, but he was sick of her questions and suspicious of her motives. Was she trying to butter him up? If she couldn't order her way out of spending time in a house with a pig, she was going to try to charm her way out of it? She was a woman far too used to getting her own way.

To end the conversation, he picked up her bags, which were numerous and heavy, and made his way up her aunt's walkway, recognizing that he was trying very hard to look like the weight was not staggering. It was a form of male preening that he wanted to curb instantly, before it got out of control. He deliberately dropped one of the bags.

"Hey! What if that has my perfume in it?" When he glanced back, she had picked up the bag, or tried to, and was dragging it along beside her. He resisted the urge to help her with it. Maybe that would teach her not to pack quite so heavily!

Rand watched Chelsea's face carefully as they went in the back door of her aunt's home.

For a house that a pig felt welcome in, it was cute, clean and cozy. As they entered the kitchen, Benjamin Franklin ambled over from a dog dish with his name on it to a bedraggled little bath mat that disappeared under his bulk when he lay down with a satisfied grunt.

"He thinks he's still a baby," Hetta said affectionately. "He's had that little scrap of mat since he could fit in the palm of my hand."

"Isn't a pig a rather unusual pet?" Chelsea asked, a little stiffly.

Her aunt shrugged. "I'm an unusual person."

He saw that Chelsea was not comfortable with unusual people. But Rand thought meeting a few unusual people—people outside of the circle she ran with, *real* people—would be good for her. Then he reminded himself, sternly, that what was good for Chelsea King was no concern of his beyond her physical safety.

Hetta brought lemonade out of the fridge and poured three frosty glasses. From the first sip he knew it was freshly squeezed. He closed his eyes in appreciation, not feeling nearly so unhappy with this situation as he had earlier. This was just what his bruised soul needed—a few weeks refuge in the heart of Americana.

He opened his eyes to see Chelsea examining her glass for smudges and darting wary looks at the pig. Then she looked at him. She wasn't quite as fond of the idea of a week or two out of the mainstream as he was. The pig had clinched it.

"Don't even think it," he told her.

"What?" she said with feigned innocence.

He gave her a level look and took another long, appreciative draw of his lemonade. She had not touched hers. Probably afraid the pig used the dishes.

"You probably couldn't even find the highway from here," he warned her. He knew immediately it had been the wrong thing to say. She was going to take that as a challenge. He sighed. The holiday was not going to be nearly as relaxing he had allowed himself to hope, however momentarily. He was going to have to sleep with one eye open, which was nothing new, and keep the car keys in the palm of his hand.

"What do you have for a vehicle?" he asked Hetta casually. *And where are the keys?*

"I don't drive," she said. "Hate it."

"Ahh." He couldn't have been more pleased. He glanced at Chelsea. If she was going to sneak off , didn't she know the rules? She should be trying to lull him into a false sense of security, make him think she'd accepted that she was staying here for a while.

But of course, she didn't know how to play that game. It was his game. She was innocent to the subtleties and rules. She was far more innocent than she was trying to look with her sophisticated style and worldly ways.

Which was why she could not win. Not against him. He had said goodbye to innocence long ago.

Chelsea waited until the house was silent. The darkness out here in the country was so complete she wondered if her escape plan was such a good idea.

But really, she'd been here less than eight hours and she'd had enough.

Aside from the pig, farm life, as she had suspected, was not for her. Her aunt had a black and white television, something Chelsea had never seen before. The TV received, barely, two flickering channels. The house had a rotary dial phone, also a museum piece, one that apparently Rand was familiar with, as he had removed some part and rendered it useless. There was no Internet connection, no stereo, not even a dishwasher. There was absolutely nothing here except the chickens.

With obvious pride her aunt had shown off her chicken coops to Rand and Chelsea. "I keep a few laying hens," Aunt Hetta had said proudly. "This is Helga, Gerta, Alberta, Francesca…" Her aunt's idea of a few was about four zillion poultry pals. Most of them with names. They smelled atrocious.

"Foul things," Chelsea had whispered to Rand, who pretended not to hear her and seemed unoffended by the smell.

Chelsea decided she was never eating chicken again. From the look on Aunt Hetta's face, there was no chance of being served chicken here, thank God, or pork. Eggs were a different story, and now that Chelsea had seen where they came from and how they looked when they came from there, she wasn't sure she could eat anything with eggs in it again, either.

Oh well, strict vegetarianism was in vogue right now anyway.

But none of that had made Chelsea's departure imperative.

No, it was that, after the tour of the chicken coop and

a sumptuously good dinner of homemade meat pies, her aunt had wanted Chelsea to read aloud.

"My vision is not what it used to be," she said, "and I miss my murder mysteries. Chelsea do you think—"

Chelsea could read, of course. But she could not read well, particularly out loud. She'd looked at the thick novel her aunt held out so hopefully and felt her stomach do a somersault.

"Oh, not tonight," she'd said breezily. "Exhausted!"

Her aunt's disappointment was palpable. "Perhaps tomorrow then," she said with quiet dignity.

"I'll read to you," Rand said, sending Chelsea a murderous look.

"Would you?" Her aunt exclaimed. "How wonderful. You'll love this book. James Kelton-Gross, *Where Evil Waltzes*."

Chelsea looked at her aunt in amazement. She looked like the least likely person to enjoy a book with that title! And Rand looked like the least likely person to read it to her. Yet, there they were, settling in on her worn living room furniture. Chelsea found herself wanting to hear the story, too, wanting to hear the mellowness of his voice as he read. Even the pig shuttled into the living room for storytime.

She was excluded and under the worst possible circumstances. Everyone thought she was a mean, selfish person. Why did that matter so much to her? Who cared if Rand thought she was a spoiled monster? She was leaving before he, or anyone else, found out the truth.

She had checked her wallet for cash when she finally made it to the privacy of a tiny bedroom under a severely sloped ceiling. Not much. She rarely used cash.

"A hundred and fifty dollars should be enough to get to a phone that has not been dismantled and to get out of town."

She said it out loud so to block out his voice, deep, self-assured, so masculine it made her feel shivery. But it didn't really work. Pathetically she put her ear to the air vent, hoping to hear some of the story.

She could hear Rand reading, her aunt's occasional appreciative gasp, but she couldn't hear enough of the actual words to grasp the plot. She leaped up and paced restlessly. *Plan*, she ordered herself, but her mind did not think in a nice orderly fashion.

She could walk down the road until she found civilization or a phone. From there it would be simple. Her friends would help her. But how long could she impose? She couldn't expect them to support her, and her father had made it very clear that she was cut off.

If he didn't come around, what was she going to do? Get a job?

The thought was not a pleasant one. She didn't exactly have marketable skills; she'd been a washout in school. She supposed she could endorse products or something equally distasteful. A reality series might be fun—as long as it didn't involve pigs or chickens. What if she had to memorize a script? The thought brought a cold feeling to the pit of her stomach.

Why was her father doing this to her?

She remembered how pale he had looked and how frail and, she felt a shiver of apprehension. He would never deliberately hurt her. What if she should stick this out, just to please him, just to see if there was something about this experience that she needed?

"Oh, and what are you going to tell them tomorrow when you don't want to read?" she chided herself. *Exhausted* would only work once. Could she pretend to splash something toxic in her eyes? No! If only she had a caramel latte and a cell phone.

The minutes ticked by with infuriating slowness. Was Rand going to read to her aunt all night? Finally the house grew blessedly quiet.

Chelsea waited and waited. And waited. It helped her pass time to think of Rand's expression of helpless fury when he woke up in the morning and found her gone. Couldn't find the highway, indeed. Every road led to a highway eventually, didn't it?

Perhaps he would be fired then.

She didn't really want to feel responsible for anyone's misfortune, but with his arrogance and self-confidence—not to mention his skill with languages—he would probably not be unemployed for long.

"La takhafii," she said to herself. "Don't be frightened."

The mantra would buoy her courage for the small adventure ahead. It was a beautiful phrase. It felt as if she might never forget it, which was another good reason to go. She didn't want to be around a man who could make a single foreign phrase seem so unforgettable.

She told herself she would wait until two, but at one in the morning, she could wait no longer. Her whole body was screaming with delicious anticipation. Really, her escape was proving more fun than she'd thought it would be.

She opened her bedroom door and snugged one carefully chosen travel bag over her shoulder. The door creaked a little and so did the stairs, but not enough to wake anyone. She stopped at the kitchen when she heard deep snores.

At first she thought Rand was sleeping down here. She loved it that the self-composed man snored like that. Then she realized those nearly human sounds were coming from the pig. Benjamin did not awake as she went by even though she crashed into a kitchen chair. She caught it before it made too much noise, and the pig only grunted.

She hurried out the door, which was not locked. An unlocked door in this day and age? There were obviously places that were simpler than what she was used to.

It was brighter outside than it had been indoors. The stars winked with astonishing abundance in an inky sky, and the moon was close to full. She stood on the porch for a moment, getting her bearings. The air smelled ripe with the scent of the nearby woods.

What if someone came along while she was walking in the dark? She was always aware that she was vulnerable in ways other people weren't. Because of her high profile, she was vulnerable even in ways her sisters were not. She had not, until this point in her life, lived in a world where her doors could be left unlocked.

The fear was not enough to stop her, though. *La takhafii,* she reminded herself, and she stepped off the porch.

A voice whispered to her in a deep and sensual growl. *"Masa 'al-kheir, ya ukhtii."*

He was so close, his breath stirred the hair on her neck. She stifled a shriek, not wanting to wake her aunt, and whirled on him. She crashed into his solid mass. His arms steadied her so that she wouldn't fall off the steps.

He smelled of heaven, as if his skin had absorbed some of the fading golden rays of the sunset. Then the contact was gone. The whole thing happened so fast it really had no right to take her breath away.

"Are you going somewhere?" he asked in English, his tone polite.

"Of course not. It was hot in my room. I couldn't sleep. I came out to admire the stars."

"With your travel bag?" he asked smoothly.

"I am not going to be treated like a prisoner," she said huffily.

"I would regret it if I had to treat you in that manner." The same polite tone, but the steel running through it was unmistakable.

She shivered, though it was not cold outside.

"Come sit on the swing."

A suggestion or an order? What would he do if she kept moving down the steps, ignored him, went on her way? Would he physically restrain her? Her cheeks caught fire at the thought. She sat on the swing, cursing herself for her docility.

His weight settled beside her. If she moved an inch her arm would be touching his. There was that scent again, heady, masculine, drugging.

"I hate it here," she said.

"Why?"

In the dark, his voice sounded almost gentle. It would be easy to believe that maybe he cared about her as more than a job.

But of course he didn't. As it had turned out, a job was all she had been to her past bodyguard. Winslow had moved onto something else with barely a warning, with a goodbye that didn't sum up all the years they'd spent together, the affection she had for him.

"There's nothing to do. A pig lives in the house. My aunt is…eccentric." *I might have to read, and I stumble over words like a third grade student tackling Shakespeare.*

"Benjamin seems rather meticulous in his hygiene habits," he said.

She heard the faint smile in his voice. "I don't like people laughing at me," she said.

"My apologies." He didn't sound the least sorry, of course. "Your aunt is very old and I suspect not as strong as she once was. There's lots to do."

"Like what?"

"You could help her."

"Help her with what?"

"Her chickens. The garden. The fence looks like it needs a coat of paint."

"Are you kidding?"

"I wasn't, no."

"The chickens smell bad! I can't be around them. I don't even think I can eat eggs anymore. And the garden? I wouldn't know the difference between a weed and a carrot, quite frankly. And do I look like somebody who knows how to paint a fence?"

"It's not rocket science."

Learning the alphabet wasn't rocket science, either, but she'd had a devil of a time doing it.

He was silent for a long time. "I don't think you have a very good idea of what you are capable of doing."

How dare he judge her? She'd learned through a great many failures that her capabilities were very different from everyone else's. She'd found, finally, a place where she fit in, where no one even knew she had trouble reading, where it didn't matter! If she looked like she led a useless, frivolous life so what? People admired her! They didn't judge her for her failings.

Still, didn't she, sometimes, in rare moments of contemplation, think, *Chelsea, what are you here for? There's got to be more to life than a party.*

She shrugged off the uncomfortable thoughts. "I don't want to be on this farm," she said. "This is not my life."

"It is your life for right now."

"Can't you talk to my father? Tell him this isn't working? I mean you can tag along in my other life, can't you? If that's your job now. What is your job, anyway? Are you temporary? Permanent?"

"Definitely temporary," he said.

"Well, that's a big surprise," she said coolly. Why did her heart fall, traitorously, as if she cared?

"Give it a week. It means a lot to your dad that you have this experience. If you can't stand it, I'll talk to your father and see if we can work out something else."

A week? She was hoping that was the longest her father wanted her to stay. But, Rand was being fair. She could see that, reluctantly. Besides, it did mean a lot to her dad. And he had never, ever been unreasonable with her.

"Okay," she said, but not happily.

"Really. Give it a chance, Chelsea. See what life here has to offer. Make the best of where you've been led."

She sighed. "I usually don't go to bed until three or four in the morning. What can I do at night?"

"Read a book?"

"I don't like gory stories."

"I've got a couple of novels with me."

"As if you and I would share the same taste in reading material!" How much easier to manufacture that sharp, haughty tone than say, *I can't read very well.*

"Watch TV?" he suggested, apparently unoffended by her tone.

"Two channels. Both off the air."

"I know a wicked card game," he said.

The invitation astonished her. "Really? I'd love to learn it! Oh, I was humiliated at the celebrity poker tournament last year. Humiliated." Of course, given her difficulty with new situations, she should have never agreed to be in it. But if she could learn a few basics, maybe this year would not be quite so terrible.

"I probably have a thing or two I could teach you."

The statement hung in the night. She bet he did have a thing or two he could teach her.

She could see the moonlight playing off the sensuous line of his lips, and her stomach did a traitorous dip. The thing it had done when she had seen him remove his shirt earlier. The thing she would most like to learn from him had nothing to do with cards, either.

Where had that dangerous thought come from?

"Never mind," she said hastily. She suddenly remembered she had trouble differentiating between sixes and nines, spades and clubs. "I'm sure you need to get some sleep."

"I won't be able to sleep if you're not."

"Don't you trust me?"

"No." A hint of a smile playing off those lips took the barb out of the words.

"Okay," she said. "Cards it is." And she flounced off

the porch swing before the moonlight made her think any other wayward thoughts about his lips. Focusing on the difference between sixes and nines should take just about every ounce of her concentration, anyway.

Chapter Three

Dumb, Rand thought, to offer to be Chelsea King's entertainment committee. What was it about her that overcame his normal sense of control and made him make a spontaneous—and utterly ridiculous—suggestion like that? He knew a wicked card game, indeed.

Even the fact that he'd used the word wicked should have warned him—and her—that cards were not the only thing on his mind.

Oh, he knew what it was that was helping him take leave of his senses. Hair turned more silver by rays of moonlight. Eyes that had flashed with heat and promise when he'd said he could teach her a thing or two. Lips that could teach *him* a thing or two.

They were a man and a woman alone together, if you didn't count the pig and the aunt upstairs sleeping. The simple truth: They were way too aware of each other in *that* way.

That way that could get a man in deep, deep trouble, make him totally lose his edge, not to mention his mind.

Once they were in the kitchen and had turned on the light, he could see that she had her hair tied back with a black ribbon and that she was dressed in black, like a Hollywood cat burglar. The turtleneck top molded her slender frame; the hip hugging flared black pants showed every delectable curve of her. He was a soldier home from the wars, tired, his soul weary, not in any kind of shape for this new kind of battle.

"Uh, on second thought," he said. "I think I better catch up on some other stuff." He could try reading the file on her. Why did he suddenly care who the hell Barry was?

But she was rummaging around in a kitchen drawer. She had already pulled out a knitting needle, a tape measure, three spools of thread and a map. "Aha," she said triumphantly, showing him the cards she'd unearthed. "Just a couple of hands. Poker. So I won't completely embarrass myself next year."

Okay, so the *wicked* part was out. That was good.

He couldn't let her out of his sight anyway, not while she was awake, with her travel bag still packed and still dressed in black.

Part of him knew he was rationalizing. But the other part of him couldn't get over her hair. Didn't she know it would practically glow in the dark on a night like this? Did she know how beautiful it looked against the black backdrop of her sweater? She must have seen him looking at her hair, because she flipped it over her shoulder. Self-conscious? Or totally conscious of the effect that would have on any red-blooded man?

It had been dumb to suggest this game. Dumber, though, to make a big deal of backing out now. She was a girl used to having way too much power, and he was just going to have to suck it up and not allow her to have any over him.

Besides, nighttime for him was peppered with restless dreams. He dreaded sleep.

She sat at the table, and he pulled out the chair across from her. After watching her clumsy effort to shuffle, he relieved her of the deck. The cards were old, naturally marked by folds and wear spots, small tears and watermarks. He made sure to shuffle the cards in a very understated way, not doing anything fancy that might alert her to the fact she was in his arena now. Though he thought any man sharing a table with her who thought it was *his* arena was probably only kidding himself.

"I'll deal. Straight poker? Two card draw?"

She focused intensely on her cards, not even noticing he was dealing from pretty much anywhere he wanted in the deck.

He dealt her the beginnings of a full house. "Do you know the basic hands?"

She nodded. She had her cards way too far out from her, and she leaned back, a classic sign of someone with a good hand—relaxed, not tense.

She tossed two cards down. She'd kept her pair of tens and a queen.

He dealt her another ten and a two. Her face lit up like the fourth of July. If he hadn't already known she had a stellar hand, he would know now.

Well, that explained why she had been humiliated at the celebrity poker tournament. He played a few hands, just to get a read on her. Though it looked like she was concentrating with all her might, concentration was obviously not her strong point. She mistook sixes for nines, once. Another time she presented a flush of clubs that had a spade in it. It was impossibly easy to read what she had in her hand from her facial expressions. He hoped she would be this easy to read the next time she planned to take off.

"Want to play for something?" he asked casually, smoothly.

"Sure. How about a hundred dollars a hand?"

She said that naturally, as if that was a small bet to her.

"Ah, I had something else in mind."

She raised her eyebrows. Something flashed in her eyes, before she blushed and reminded him how young she really was.

"Not that," he said dryly.

"I didn't say anything," she protested.

Yes, you did. "A week. No matter what happens, or how much you hate it, you'll stay put for a week. No, um, midnight strolls."

"I already agreed to that," she said huffily.

"I think you had your fingers crossed."

"Okay. Okay. It's a deal. But what if I win?" she said.

No chance of that happening. "Name your bet."

"We leave first thing in the morning?"

If he agreed to that, she'd probably figure out he had a thing or two up his sleeve that made her ever collecting on that bet an impossibility. "Not that. Anything else."

"Anything?" she said wickedly.

He did have a way of letting his guard down with her around. "Within reason," he amended.

"What you think is reasonable and what I think is reasonable are probably two different things."

"Probably," he agreed dryly.

She thought for a moment, her brow crinkled with intense concentration. Then she brightened. "You have to read to my aunt again. Not me."

He regarded her thoughtfully. "Okay, but why that? I mean you could have really had some fun with this bet—chicken coops that need cleaning, ladies underwear, kissing the pig."

She laughed, and her eyes lit with pure devilment. He liked her laugh, throaty and real, not a Hollywood laugh at all.

"Ladies underwear!," she gasped. "Oh, my God, I missed my chance. Can I change it?"

She wasn't going to win, anyway. "Sure," he said, dead-pan.

Now she did look a teensy bit suspicious. "Never mind. I'll stick with the reading. Maybe next time I'll reveal my cruelly ingenious side to you."

It was his turn to laugh. But he realized she had carefully—maybe even craftily—avoided answering his question. Why didn't she want to read to her aunt? Was it possible she was just easily bored? She was obviously not as insensitive as he would have liked to think, because she wanted *someone* to read to her aunt, even if it wasn't going to be her.

"Best of ten hands?" he said.

She nodded, eager to get started. He let her win the first four, though technically she should have lost the last hand. She mixed up a six with a nine again. He pretended he didn't notice, and she sincerely seemed not to see it. It was going to be very difficult to make her start losing, when watching her win was so much fun. Her hair started to fall out of the ribbon; her cheeks were flushed with excitement. Every time she won, she threw her cards on the table with a flourish and did an unself-conscious "happy" dance around the kitchen.

She either really loved winning or really hated reading. Or, perhaps there was a third option. Perhaps Chelsea King was just filled with a naive and delight-ful enthusiasm for life that was surprising given who she was. Even more surprising was how it touched him, given the jaded soul that he was.

He realized she had something—the "it" factor the press coupled with her name at every opportunity—and that she would have had it even if she was not a King. She wasn't so intensely popular only because she was beautiful and rich. Behind her mask, he glimpsed in-triguing qualities—playfulness, humor. And a kind of unconscious sensuality that was riveting.

He found himself wishing she wasn't a King, wishing that the circumstances were different. But he killed those thoughts like weeds that could take over a good field, and began to change the direction of the card game.

By hand number nine, she wasn't looking nearly so happy. Her expression was one of furious concentration and helpless frustration. The look was, unfortunately, nearly as endearing as her happy dances had been.

Suddenly she threw down her cards and folded her arms over her chest. She gave him the full benefit of the wattage of that gold-green gaze. "You're cheating."

He felt a little ripple of shock. Had the fact that she

couldn't tell the difference between a six and a nine led him to believe she was not smart? Maybe one person in a thousand would have been able to tell he was cheating.

"I am?" he asked, playing the innocent, while he re-aligned his assessment of her. *Complicated*, was what he came up with. She seemed superficial, but she wanted someone to read to her aunt. She seemed playful, and yet a certain shrewdness lay just beneath her distracting exterior.

"I know you are cheating. I don't care, really. I mean, we're staying here for the week whether I win or not. But I think, just as a matter of honor, you should read to my aunt."

"Agreed," he said solemnly.

"See. I knew you were cheating."

He inclined his head, faint acknowledgment that she had caught him red-handed so to speak.

But she wasn't done with him yet. "What I want to know is how. That's what I want to learn."

"How to cheat at cards?" he asked, dumbfounded. What possible application would that have in her life?

"Please?" She leaned toward him and blinked.

Who could resist that?

"The deck's bad," he explained to her. "You would never see a deck like this in a real poker game."

He showed her the marks that had helped him identify everything in her hand, every time. He didn't admit to a little sneaky dealing. He'd save that for tomorrow night. Which meant he was thinking, crazily, there was going to be another night just like this one.

How much temptation did he think he could handle?

On the other hand, while he'd played cards with her

he'd learned things about her that he might need to know. Oh, sure, he told himself. That she was *complicated*. And smart, he reminded himself. Way smarter than he had given her credit for. That was important information. More than important. Essential.

"Even if the deck hadn't been marked," he told her, "your face and your body language were telegraphing a whole lot of information about your hand."

"They were?"

"This is your *I'm holding three-aces* look." He made his eyes go round and leaned back so far his chair nearly fell over. He blinked rapidly several times.

"Stop it!" she said, throwing a card at him, but she was laughing again. "I never had three aces!"

"Well, if you had, that's what you would have looked like."

"You're being mean."

"You have to be mean to play cards. Ruthless. Heartless. Those things come naturally to me. I'm not sure they can be taught."

"You're not mean," she said softly.

"That's not what you thought after I, um, disposed of your cell phone," he reminded her.

"Just because you can do mean things doesn't make you mean," she said.

"Well, the distinction seems a little fuzzy to me." He didn't like this one little bit. He didn't like the way she was looking at him, as if she could see something in him that no one had seen for a very long time.

"Welcome to The Art of Cheating at Cards 101," he said, deciding not to save anything for tomorrow night, after all. Tomorrow night she was going to her room, and he was reading the file that he should be reading right now. Right after he read to her aunt, that was. Tomorrow night, and every night after that, it was going to be strictly business between the two of them. But tonight, he would give himself this small gift. He would bask in the look in her eyes that said he was not the things that he had done.

So, with Benjamin Franklin snoring gently in the background, Chelsea King, socialite, learned to play cards from a man who had learned most of his own tricks in a world very far from hers. In a world where mean people did mean things, and there was no distinction between who they were and what they did.

Actually what she learned was how to cheat at cards. He did his best to show her how to mark a deck, how to count it. She was an eager student, though dismal at keeping numbers straight. Patterns eluded her completely. She had no aptitude for small details, and she even struggled with larger ones, such as the difference between a spade and a club.

"Don't make that face," he told her, again.

"What face?"

"You're smiling."

"I am not!"

He was becoming an expert on her lips, unfortunately, and that little twitch of satisfaction might not be a smile, exactly, but it was close enough.

"Keep your face blank."

She stuck out her tongue at him.

"Don't do that, either. I can tell you have a great hand when you get mischievous."

She threw down her hand.

It stank.

She stuck out her tongue at him again. "See? You're not so smart."

And he better remember that when he got too cocky, thinking he had her number, when obviously getting Chelsea King's number would take a lifetime of fairly intensive investigation.

"Okay," he said. "Let me show you something else, but don't use any of this at the celebrity tournament."

He showed her the top card on the deck. "I don't want you to have that card, obviously," he said. He dealt. She picked up her cards, and her mouth formed an "O" of astonishment.

He sighed. She was never going to get the blank look down pat. Never. Not if he had a million years to show it to her.

A million years with Chelsea King. Forever.

He did not want to be thinking of this girl and forever in the same sentence.

"How did you do that?" she demanded. "What happened to the king?"

He lifted his sleeve and revealed the missing king to her.

Her mouth formed that adorable "O" again before she caught his look and snapped it shut.

"Where did you learn that kind of stuff?" she asked him, as if a little sleight of hand made him Houdini.

He was silent for a long time. It was late. He was tired. She seemed like the softest thing he had ever seen. He heard himself saying, "In the same kinds of places you learn to speak foreign languages. The kinds of places that give a man nightmares that would make him rather play cards all night than sleep."

He saw her holding her breath, wanting him to tell her, to trust her. He was going to reveal some secret part of himself if he didn't smarten up right now. With the dawn coming up, he was going to tell her something he had told no one. He was going to tell her about the worst night of his life.

But just then there was a heavy clomping on the stairs, and Hetta burst into the kitchen, fully dressed in coveralls and a floppy hat. She put her hands on her hips and looked at them approvingly. "I like people who are up at the first crack of light. Chelsea, do you want to come with me for eggs?"

The moment, the desire for confession, evaporated, and he felt relief sweep over him. He stretched and tossed down his cards. "I'll come with you," he said to Hetta, but his eyes never left Chelsea's. He said, "*Sabah al-warada*. It means good morning."

Rand trailed Hetta King out the door, deeply shocked at himself. If Hetta had not arrived how much would he have told Chelsea?

He gave his head a shake. And why did he want to speak to her in the pure poetry of the Arabic language? Last night, when he had caught her sneaking from the house he had greeted her in Arabic, aware of his own hesitation when he used *ukhtii*—my sister—a greeting for an acquaintance that emphasized respect. His first choice had been a more intimate greeting.

He'd told her, just now, that *sabah al-warada* meant good morning, and it did, but it was not the typical greeting, which was *sabah al-kheir* or morning of goodness. No, he'd greeted her with morning of roses. He looked to the sky, the dawn painting mountains in shades of pink and orange and red. But he was kidding himself if he thought it was the morning light that had brought the phrase to mind. No, it was her, spending the night with her, and not exactly in the way a man wanted to spend the night with a beautiful woman.

Playing cards with her, teaching her those cheats, had been fun. She was amazingly quick and interested, her laugh was ready and contagious. No wonder the whole world couldn't get enough of her. She had some ephemeral quality of spirit that was wonderful.

I have to get off this job, he realized. Playing cards with her had been a reprieve from his own demons, but he still had not studied her file. Wouldn't that have been a more professional use for his insomnia? Those letters posed a very real threat to her safety. Was he going to trust another man to protect her, especially now that he'd seen laughter stain her cheeks to the color of roses?

He sighed and followed Hetta through the door to her chicken coop. Without preamble she handed him a shovel.

"Put that good strong back to use," she said.

He looked at the shovel and at the mountain of manure collecting under the chicken pens. He sighed. He was in hell. But for a man in hell he was aware, an hour later, that he was whistling contentedly as he lent his back to the labor at hand and cursed the chickens softly. In Arabic.

Then he looked at Hetta, who had just finished feeding and watering her flock. The contentment was gone as suddenly as air from a pin-pricked balloon.

Sarah Jane McKenzie plopped down on her sofa, exhausted. The exhaustion did not prevent her from noticing the poor repair of the couch or from comparing this depressing room in a Hollow Gap, Virginia, rooming house to what she had left behind, her delightful little apartment over the garage at Kingsway.

She felt tears sting her eyes, but she furiously pushed them down.

This was what she deserved. Jake King had been kind to her, and in return she had stolen from him. She had rationalized it, because she knew a truth he did not. She was his granddaughter. Why hadn't she just told him? There had been opportunities.

"Because you're dumb as a sack of hammers," she told herself. But she knew that wasn't the truth. She'd been scared, plain and simple. Scared he wouldn't react well, if he'd wanted to know his granddaughter, he would have answered her letter. Sarah had been scared enough that she had helped herself to souvenirs, the only legacy she might ever get from her grandfather. Now, she didn't even have those silly things: ashtrays and candlesticks. What had she been thinking?

The smell of cooking clung to her uniform from the diner, but she wanted to just watch TV, for a minute, before she went down the hall to the shower. The late, late news was on. Bad news for people who had children in that war, and there were lots of them from around here that did. A possible cure for a disease that Sarah had never heard of. And then, shots from the wrap party for the film *The Third Entity*, which starred Chelsea's friend, Barry MacIntosh. She leaned forward, hoping to see Chelsea.

But instead Barry was with another girl and the announcers' voice said, "Notably absent from this occasion is Barry MacIntosh's usual escort, Chelsea King. Her friends are mum, but rumor has it she may be in treatment for substance abuse or an eating disorder."

Sarah stared at the TV. How could they say such a thing? Chelsea did not have a substance abuse problem or an eating disorder! But was something wrong with Chelsea? Where there was smoke there could be fire. Chelsea had been talking about the parties that would surround that movie even before Sarah left Kingsway. Why would she miss it? What if she was sick?

It was none of Sarah's business, now, she knew that. And yet she was up and off her sofa in the blink of an eye. There was a phone in the downstairs hallway, but it had been blocked from making long distance calls. With her pockets full of change from her tips, she ran out onto the dark street to the corner pay phone. She dialed his number from the business card he had given her, his home number jotted on the back. The numbers were nearly worn off the card because she had handled it so much, but they were committed to memory, anyway.

Cameron would know if Chelsea was okay.

As she dialed the last number and followed the instructions to deposit coins, she came to her senses. She couldn't talk to Cameron! He wouldn't answer the phone anyway. It was the middle of the night. If he did answer, would he be able to figure out where she was? That's what he did. Figured things out, kind of like a private detective. This was a stupid idea. She went to hang up the phone, but just before it came to rest in the cradle, she heard a voice, deep, male, groggy.

"Hello?"

As if caught in a spell, she lifted the receiver back to her ear.

"Hello?' he said again.

Don't answer she ordered herself. "Hello, Cameron."

"Sarah?" All the sleepiness was gone from his voice. She pictured him sitting up in bed, reaching for a lamp, the light spilling over the naked beauty of his chest and arms.

"Sarah?"

"I just saw a thing about Chelsea on the news. That she wasn't at Barry's party tonight. Is she okay, Cameron?"

Stupid. She was crying.

"Sarah, where are you?"

Crying harder at the gentle note in his voice, almost as if he didn't care that she was a thief. "Is Chelsea okay?" she managed to choke out.

"Chelsea's fine. Are you?"

She hated that it sounded as if he was really concerned. She wanted to tell him the truth. No, she was not okay. She was never going to be okay. She had tasted finer things, she had seen how life could be. Being back in that diner—serving coffee and greasy breakfast all day and into the night, having her bottom slapped, and counting her tips—that was a life sentence. One she deserved, though even murderers didn't always get life sentences.

"I'm okay," she said through tears.

"Are you crying? Dammit, Sarah."

She said nothing. She ordered herself to hang up, but she didn't, wanting, *needing* to hear his voice. Something she could hang on to tomorrow when the coffee spilled and the tables didn't get wiped quickly enough, when she got stiffed because the cook had burned the bacon.

"Where are you? Sarah, we need to talk."

Oh, sure, they needed to talk. About her stealing from people who had trusted her. Maybe Cameron would even put her in jail. As head of security that was his job, wasn't it? Would jail be better than the café and her living quarters? Cleaner? Less pats on the bottom?

"Sarah, talk to me."

His voice was low, pleading, *tender*.

"Tell Chelsea—" She stopped, hesitated, then slowly hung up the phone. She pressed her forehead against the glass booth. No, she could not start playing that game. She could not allow herself to believe that she could still have contact with them, phone every now and then to leave a message. No. There could be no messages, no more concern. She had made her choice, and now she had to live with it.

Still, she wished she had said it. *Tell Chelsea I'm sorry.*

Chapter Four

"*S*abah al-warada," Chelsea sang softly to herself, as she scooped up the cards off her aunt's kitchen table. It was totally unfair that the man spoke in poetry. He said it only meant good morning, but it *felt* like more than that. It felt like it meant a morning full of promise, of delight.

How could she read so much into one little phrase? How could she read so much into Rand when really, he said so little, revealed so little. But his eyes spoke Arabic. Mystery and passion and poetry lived in the startling green pools of his eyes.

She put one of the cards in the palm of her hand. How could she hide something that was bigger than her hand? Still, she tried to get the card under the sleeve of her sweater. It didn't work. It didn't work the first time she did it, and it wasn't working the fifteenth time she tried it, either.

Where did a person learn things like that? But more important, how did they find the time to practice it, over and over, until something terribly hard looked easy, until a motion so obvious became invisible?

He had been about to tell her. She knew, instinctively, he was a closed man who revealed things about himself stingily. She knew, instinctively, he was a man who had secrets he had never shared. She knew, instinctively, he had fought battles that had left wounds on his soul that put the ones on his face to shame. And she had known, instinctively, he had been about to do the rarest of things. Share something with her—trust her.

Then fate had intervened, in the form of her aunt.

Chelsea went to the window. She allowed herself to feel, again, the faint tingle of anticipation that she had felt when he had looked at her so long and hard. Chelsea was aware of feeling faintly light-headed. Not just with fatigue, but with a sense of discovery. She had never really been a person who knew things *instinctively*. And yet she knew things about him. Her heart felt things about him.

It was scary and exciting, exhilarating and confusing.

Was it possible she'd had more fun sitting in this simple kitchen playing cards than she'd had doing many much more glorious and glamorous things? Last night the cast of Barry's movie had their wrap party. Was she sorry to have missed it?

"Not really," she admitted out loud. The thought bothered her. That was her life, her *real* life. Was it so ungratifying that one night of playing poker could make her want something else? Something deeper?

"Deeper. Playing poker with a card cheat would

hardly qualify!" she told herself huffily. She turned on the radio to avoid the direction of her thoughts.

"He's charming you," she told herself. "He's charming you to get his own way." Rand Peabody wanted no disappearing acts, and he would do whatever it took to achieve that.

Was it true? He seemed like a man incapable of charm in the way she understood the word, and she understood it. She always had to be suspicious of people. Who was authentic and who was not? Who really liked her, and who just wanted to be close to her because they enjoyed her fame, her status, her money? What if it wasn't her *instinct* reacting to him at all? What if it was something more base? Chemical? Hormonal? What if the fact that she wanted to taste his lips—and she did—was warping all her other judgments?

"Introspection," she reminded herself, "gives me a headache. And so does infatuation." She was quite pleased with herself for coming up with those words since vocabulary had never been one of her strong points.

She froze suddenly and turned to the radio. Had she heard her name?

"And now for entertainment news, featuring Betsy Blinkoff."

Betsy was talking, in that in-the-know voice of hers, about the wrap party for *The Last Entity*. She said it had been a wonderfully creative affair where the star-shaped canapés had been served by little people in alien suits, who had upstaged the attending stars and celebs.

"I should have been there," Chelsea said mutinously, but somehow she could not conjure up any real regret, little people in alien suits not withstanding. It sounded like it might have been a waste of the Marchesa dress.

"Noticeably absent from the event was Chelsea King," Betsy said, her voice dropping an octave that foreshadowed something really *juicy*. "Rumors are flying that she is at the Betty Ford clinic, but my sources say differently."

The Betty Ford Clinic? Chelsea rolled her eyes. She knew she should be used to this by now, but somehow she never was. She did not use drugs, and she drank very sparingly. She most certainly did not qualify for entrance to the famed drug rehab center.

"Chelsea King is definitely not at the Betty Ford Clinic," Betsy announced with great and enthusiastic authority.

Chelsea chewed a nail, absurdly eager to find out her own whereabouts from Betsy. "My sources say she's in the world famous Marguerite O'Hare Clinic that treats—" dramatic pause "—eating disorders!!"

Chelsea's mouth fell open. An eating disorder? Where did people get this stuff? Why was it okay to make things up about her? She itched to set the record straight! She glared at the disabled phone. Rand had to have a cell phone somewhere! He had to. People in this day and age did not live without cell phones. She would find it, and then she would call that stupid bovine so aptly named Betsy. Then of course she would phone her friends, because even your best friends sometimes heard news like that and didn't know what to believe.

She stood at a turning place, where her old life tugged at her with bonds made of steel. No introspection. No infatuation. Safe, in its way, because shooting down a few rumors before they gathered wind was much easier than shooting down the feeling she got in the pit of her stomach every time she thought of Rand's eyes twinkling with mischief when he showed her how to cheat.

She charged upstairs and found his things in a little room under the attic very similar to hers. The room was stark—a small suitcase unopened on the bed, a briefcase on the desk. There was a bottle of cologne on the dresser, and she guiltily sniffed it. A gorgeous scent. She cursed her lack of focus. She was looking for a cell phone! She had to find it before doubt made her question her right to be in his room going through his things. She reminded herself of Betsy's remarks. Filled with righteousness she moved to the desk and snapped open his briefcase.

He'd be furious if he knew. She shivered thinking of how he might look. But it was his own fault. She wouldn't be in such desperate need of a phone if he had not so heartlessly disposed of hers.

Heartless. That was what she needed to remember when she was fighting the temptation to contemplate his eyes, when she was tempted to relive words that came off his lips, words that should have no meaning at all in her world!

No cell phone in that neat briefcase. But a thick file with her name on it!

She felt as violated as the radio announcement had made her feel. Was nothing her own? Did it say, somewhere in that folder, that she had a reading disability? Was he going to read that and feel sorry for her? Or worse, feel contemptuous of her? No, he wasn't because he was never going to see it. Annoyed, she plucked the file from his briefcase. She was, she reminded herself sternly, his *job*.

She heard the back door open.

"Chelsea?"

Damn the sexiness of that voice. Her name from those lips made a chill go up and down her spine.

"Weakling," she berated herself. She raced into her own room and, feeling a certain delightful sense of power, she opened the closet, which had nothing in it, and put the file way back on the dusty shelf. Then she went down the stairs. She met him halfway. She was letting him have it about the cell phone!

"Did you know what was on the radio just now?" she asked, in a snit and prepared to let him know it. "I need a phone. Immediately."

He took her shoulders in his hands.

What she needed *immediately* suddenly seemed very confused. She looked into his eyes and saw both calm and urgency there.

"I need you to listen very carefully," he said. "Your aunt is sick. I believe she may be having a heart attack."

"Oh, my God! Where is she? Call 9-1-1! What—" She couldn't believe how much she cared about her aunt, a woman she barely knew.

"There is no 9-1-1 here."

"No 9-1-1?" Her voice came out very shrill. No 9-1-1? How was that possible? What did people do—

"I need you to be very, very calm," he said slowly, enunciating each word.

She looked into his eyes and heard that he needed her. She knew that he meant it. The panic that was trying to rise up in her stilled.

"She doesn't want to believe she's having a heart attack," he said softly, "though she is having classic symptoms, one of the most classic being denial. She hates hospitals, and she says she won't go."

Chelsea nodded that she understood.

"We're putting her in the car, and we're taking her to the hospital. Your job is to keep her calm, okay? No added stress. If she starts getting excited, divert her."

"Are you going to put her in the car against her will?" she asked, frightened.

"I hope the hell not."

But she heard that he would if he had to. He scanned her face. Chelsea nodded, to let him know she completely got the severity of the situation, and he turned and headed back down the narrow staircase. Her aunt was sitting in a rocker on the front porch. She was very pale, and her forehead was beaded with sweat.

"It's nothing," she said defiantly, as Chelsea came and knelt beside her. "A little pain in my chest."

"Come on, Hetta," Rand said. His voice was patient, but had that familiar don't-mess-with-me note of steel running through it. "Chelsea and I are taking you to the hospital."

"I won't go!" She folded her arms stubbornly over her chest.

"You are going." Each word was bitten out carefully, with the calm authority of a man used to being obeyed. But Hetta wasn't a soldier. She was an old, old woman who had done things her own way for a long time. Chelsea was startled by how she felt she *understood* her aunt. Hetta would see Rand, for all his power and presence, as a young whippersnapper, and she would be almost honor-bound to defy his attempts to order her around.

"If I'm going to die, so be it," Hetta said. "I'll die right here on my front porch. It's as good a place as any."

Rand looked as if he was going to pick up Chelsea's diminutive aunt and toss her over his shoulder, which would not be good for the stress levels they were trying to control.

Chelsea caught Rand's eye, shook her head. He glared at her. He knew what he wanted done, and he thought he knew how to do it, but he didn't. Her aunt was terrified, and she was proud.

Chelsea took Hetta's hand, and stood, drawing her aunt to her feet. "Let's just go for a little walk," she suggested, "and see if that makes you feel better."

"I suppose," Hetta said.

Chelsea walked her slowly toward the car. She felt Rand following and turned and gave him a warning look as in *Don't you dare open the door and shove*.

Rand scowled at her but backed off a few steps.

"I wonder," she said softly to Hetta, "what would happen to Benjamin if something were to happen to you?"

"I've never been in a hospital and I'm not going now." But Chelsea noticed Hetta allowed herself to be led in the direction of the car.

"What if we just went for a checkup?" Chelsea said soothingly, and then pressed home the point again. "Some people would just look at Benjamin and see pork."

Her aunt tried to stifle a gasp and she shot Benjamin a worried glance. Chelsea caught Rand's barely perceptible nod of approval. She was also not unaware that he was *surprised* that she was handling this better than he.

"I don't have insurance," Hetta said, and Chelsea exchanged another glance with Rand. It was different than the out and out no of earlier and they both knew it.

"I don't think you need to worry about that," Chelsea said. "My dad will look after you."

At first she thought it was the wrong thing to say to such a fiercely independent woman, but Hetta's insulted arguments allowed Rand to open the back door and help her aunt slide into the car.

Hetta suddenly seemed to realize where she was, and her lack of protest made Chelsea worry that the heart pains were getting worse. She wanted to scream, *hurry, for God's sake,* but she knew she had to maintain this pretense of absolute calm, for her aunt.

"I hate automobiles," Hetta said testily.

Chelsea wondered if maybe her aunt hated new situations, just like she did. Maybe it was a family disorder. She got into the car, took her aunt's hand, and was surprised when Hetta laid her head on Chelsea's shoulder.

"Tell me about Benjamin Franklin," Chelsea said. When she had been afraid of a homework assignment thinking of things that she liked had kept her from focusing on what terrified her most.

Her aunt sighed. "He's a Yorkshire pig. I used to raise them and then sell them for slaughter. Until he came along. Runt of the litter. Kind of wormed his way into my heart, he did. When the day came to ship them, he hung back from all his brothers and sisters. I looked at him, and saw he was shaking like a leaf. Like he knew.

"And then I saw the most astonishing thing I'd ever seen. He was crying. A tear was coming out his eye.

"I kept him. Never slaughtered another pig after that. They're intelligent creatures, and very, very clean, if given the chance."

As she talked about pigs, and about her beloved Benjamin, Hetta's voice grew calmer. Rand's eyes met Chelsea's in the rearview mirror, and again she could tell he was surprised she was doing such a good job of keeping her aunt's mind occupied with things other than the car ride and her heart and her imminent arrival at the hospital.

How dare he brand her such a dumb twit when he barely knew her! So much for the trust she thought he'd had in her this morning! She stuck out her tongue at him and saw him shake his head and smile, as if that was more in line with what he expected of her.

She met his eyes in the mirror, once more. There was nothing in them now except professionalism, a man who was all business. He was complicated. It would be dangerous to think she knew this man too well, it would be dangerous to trust him with too much.

Still, she knew if he wasn't there, an anchor of stability, she would be petrified with panic to find herself in this situation. Complicated or not, Rand Peabody radiated the aura of a man who handled life and death situations as a matter of course. His calm was contagious.

They were, at this moment, a team, albeit a reluctant one.

She hoped he appreciated that little detail as much as she did.

Would there be a poker game tonight?

Chelsea looked at her aunt and hoped there would be. She hoped her aunt had a case of indigestion and that they would all be going home together. Considering how badly she had wanted to leave the farm yesterday, that desire was ironic.

But it was not to be. Farewell had only a tiny, rural hospital, and in short order, they had determined her aunt had blockages in her arteries. At the minimum she would need a stint to open her heart valve.

"We're going to have to air ambulance her to a larger center."

"What a way to have my first airplane ride," Hetta groused.

But Chelsea noted Hetta was not protesting with much enthusiasm. Hetta looked small and old and very frightened in her hospital bed.

"I'm going with you," Chelsea announced.

Hetta patted Chelsea's hand. "No. I need you to look after my Benjamin and my chickens. You need to go back and do that now. Tomorrow morning is the day I always make my food bank run. You'll have to do that. They count on me."

"I think I should stay with you."

"I don't want you to," her aunt said firmly. "I need to have a talk with my Maker, by myself. And I need to know my responsibilities at home are being looked after."

"Okay," Chelsea said, reluctantly. "What do we need to do?"

"Feed and water Benjamin and the chickens. Rand, you saw how I did it this morning?"

He nodded.

"Tomorrow they serve soup at the Bounty Kitchen here in Farewell. It's on Abner Street, east of the railway tracks. My neighbor, on the south side of me, picks up the produce and then I walk into town to help make the soup. But you might as well call him and cancel since you have a car. You can deliver the goods, carrots and tomatoes, peas and potatoes out of the garden. Enough to make soup for fifty people."

Chelsea cast Rand a look. Did he know how much would make soup for fifty people? Apparently. The request didn't seem to faze him in the least. Of course, the only thing that seemed to have fazed him, since their first meeting, was Chelsea's cell phone!

"You need to help them make the soup," Hetta said. "They never have enough volunteers."

Make soup? Feed chickens? Look after a pig? Oh, her friends would think this was hilarious. Maybe there was a hidden camera somewhere!

"Okay," Chelsea said, trying to reassure her aunt, despite her doubts. "I've got it."

But her aunt, despite how sick she was, looked skeptical. "He'll help you. Won't you, Rand?"

"Yes, ma'am."

"Making soup for an army is nothing to you, is it?"

He shrugged. Hetta smiled. "I'm fine. Go make sure Benjamin's okay. He doesn't like to be left alone."

They glanced back, before leaving the room. Hetta had her hands folded together, and her eyes squinched tightly shut. From the intensity of her expression, it was apparent she thought her most ardent prayers would be necessary to keep the plane in the sky!

"Do you think anybody listens?" Chelsea asked.

"To prayers?" Rand asked, and he sounded cynical. "Yes."

He hesitated a long time, then he put his hand

lightly on her shoulder. "I think your aunt will be just fine, Chelsea."

But she was aware he had not answered her question.

Rand left his hand on her shoulder as he guided her out of the room. Given how slender she was, he might have expected her to feel frail, but instead, he felt the surprising strength in her.

Just as he had seen it during that perilously long trip to the hospital. He'd been amazed at how she'd managed to keep Hetta so calm. He'd seen his error in trying to muscle the old gal into doing what she needed to do. Chelsea had known the magic key to her aunt's cooperation would be the pig. He had missed that.

It underscored what he was finding out moment by moment—there was a whole lot more to Chelsea King than anyone would have guessed. She was not the superficial young lady who had been, just yesterday, telling anyone who would listen, *Oh, my God, I'm a prisoner.*

She had risen to this occasion and to this challenge with spunk and spirit.

They were making their way down a long corridor that led out of the hospital when a young woman pushing a cart filled with dirty dishes stopped and stared at Chelsea.

"Are you Chelsea King?" she asked breathlessly.

He could tell Chelsea was used to handling this type of thing. She smiled and moved toward the woman, her hand out. He skillfully inserted himself between Chelsea and her fan. The last thing he needed was word going through the small town, like wildfire, that they had a celebrity in their midst. Besides, Chelsea's smile looked forced, and he could see the exhaustion causing circles under her eyes.

"No, she's not," he said abruptly. "She gets asked that all the time, though." He took Chelsea's elbow and tried to move by.

The woman, who was wearing a name tag that said Candy, caught his sleeve as he went by. "It is so her! I've seen her in magazines. I just want an autograph!"

He looked at her hand on his arm, and she yanked it away. Then he shoved Chelsea, now unwilling, out the front doors of the hospital.

"Why did you do that?" she hissed at him.

He shrugged, but turned back and glared at the woman, who was following them. Until the moment her eyes met his she looked like she had every intention of pursuing them into the parking lot. Now, she stopped, and looked indignant as if she was *owed* something she had not received.

Welcome to the dark side of Chelsea's celebrity, he thought. The woman was giving him a look of pure malice. Then, a light came on in her face, and she yanked a cell phone from her pocket and aimed it at them.

Obviously the kind that took pictures. Rand did his best to shield Chelsea.

"Rand, for Pete's sake, is it so hard to be nice to people?"

"Yeah," he said. "It is."

He glanced back at the woman who was still holding her cell phone pointed at them. He cursed her silently—*yikhrub beitak*—may your house be wrecked, and he had the ill grace to hope that happened before Candy got a hold of anybody who cared about the pictures she had just captured on her phone.

He knew from the look on her face, she meant

trouble. But how much trouble? Maybe Chelsea had been right. If they'd stopped and given her the autograph, that might have been the end of it, though he doubted it. Either way, he bet that by tonight everyone in the world was going to know that Chelsea was in Farewell, Virginia.

He weighed his decision, aware that dealing with rabid fans was brand-new territory for him. Would it have been better or worse if he'd let Chelsea talk to her? Worse, he figured. Then she'd know for sure who she had seen. Now she had a bit of a doubt—a doubt that would be erased if she saw the name Hetta *King* somewhere in that hospital and put two and two together.

But Hetta was flying out soon. Candy might never be totally sure it was Chelsea King she had seen. She might never do anything about it, if she did realize it. Besides, Hetta was counting on them. *Them*. He and Chelsea, a surprising team.

He recognized emotion was playing a part in his decision, and he didn't like that one little bit.

"It doesn't hurt to be nice," Chelsea said again as she slid through the car door he held open for her.

"Hey, your aunt is sick. Obviously you aren't in the hospital for your own entertainment. You're entitled to your space, to private moments."

"I could have said hello to her. That's all she wanted."

"Yeah, to begin with."

"What does that mean?"

"And then an autograph. She even said that. And then an invitation to dinner. And then a job."

Chelsea was silent, so he knew he'd struck a nerve.

"You know who gets stalked?" he asked her.

"Famous people?" she said sarcastically.

"Yeah, famous *nice* people."

"Excuse me?"

"Stalkers choose people they perceive as *nice*. Approachable."

"Then you are in absolutely no danger of being stalked are you?"

"Absolutely none," he agreed with satisfaction. This sparring between them was much better than the bond that had been forming while they dealt with her aunt's crisis. He had to maintain a professional distance, a clear mind.

He had to.

Her life might depend on it, especially if the news was going to get out that she was in Farewell. And he was pretty sure it was.

"What makes you such an expert on stalkers?" she asked snottily.

He had to be careful how he answered. He certainly did not want to reveal to her that preparation for this job had made him an expert on that subject.

Instead he said, "I'm an expert on all things that crawl out from underneath rocks."

"How pleasant for you."

He nodded. "Yeah," he said, "it is."

"Do you have a cell phone?"

"Yeah, I do."

"May I use it?"

He had now been awake for close to thirty-six hours. Maybe that was taking the edge off his reasoning skills, because he removed the cell phone from the inner pocket of his jacket and gave it to her. No questions, no instructions. She was after all, the woman he had nearly told his deepest secrets to. She was, after all, the woman who had totally amazed him this morning when crisis had hit.

She had a strong, compassionate side that was absolutely spell-binding. And, he reminded himself, she had cast her spell on someone who now wanted to hurt her. Someone who was probably going to be one step closer to finding out where she was because of Candy.

He wasn't aware he was holding his breath, until she spoke into the cell phone, and he exhaled.

"Hi, James. I need to speak to my dad."

Moments later, in a low voice, she was giving the details of her aunt's condition to her father. She finished with an *I love you* that was so sweetly genuine that Rand felt his throat tighten. Then she closed the phone and handed it back to him. She had not told her father that he, Rand, had destroyed her cell phone and been rude to her. She had not even attempted to call any of her friends.

They were a grown man and a grown woman operating on too little sleep, a situation that invited bad decisions. They were heading back to that farm by themselves. No Hetta to chaperone them.

He didn't need a chaperone, he told himself grimly. His self-discipline was legendary. He'd tested it when he was tired before, and passed.

He slid her a look, and knew he'd never had a test like Chelsea King.

"I think," he said, after a moment, "that we should get your father to hire someone to look after the farm."

Her mouth opened in shock, and then closed stubbornly. "I can do it. We can do it. Aunt Hetta would hate strangers at her place."

"We're practically strangers," he reminded her.

"You are," she corrected him. "I'm blood."

He had a feeling that made a big difference in these mountains. Some inheritance from the strong and stubborn people of these parts ran through Chelsea's veins though she had been far removed from this world for her whole life.

"You *wanted* to go yesterday," he reminded her.

"And you didn't," she said. "Things can change in a second, never mind a whole day."

He grunted.

"Aunt Hetta has a better chance of getting well if she feels relaxed. If she knows people she trusts are looking after things. She *trusts* me."

She said this as if something sacred had been given into her keeping, and he knew it had. It made his job way more difficult, but he felt responsible for more than Chelsea. He felt responsible for Hetta, too. It was as if he'd been thrust into a family.

He was not good at families. His own, never particularly healthy, had dissolved when he was fourteen. His mother had been unable to cope with the constant pressure of all the moves his father's military career required of them. Or maybe she'd just been tired of coping, period, because she had asked Rand to stay with his father. Rand had learned the lesson that duty came before personal fulfillment.

He liked jobs that did not remind him of all that. He liked jobs where emotional distance could be kept.

The last time he'd formed an emotional attachment on a job it had all blown up. Literally. In his face. So, he should know better.

Way better.

He looked at Chelsea's face. Though Rand knew himself to be a powerful man, he knew he could not fight the determination he saw there.

They would be looking after her aunt's farm, and they would do it no matter what he had to say about it. He pondered that interesting development—that shift in control—while he drove them back to the farm.

Chapter Five

They pulled into her aunt Hetta's driveway, and Chelsea watched as Benjamin galloped off the porch to greet them. The portly pig nearly fell down the steps in his eagerness to get to the car. Chelsea was reminded of her own statement about how quickly everything could change. Just yesterday, this pig had made her scream. Today he was making her smile.

Still, she cried, "Please don't touch me," as Benjamin barreled toward her, ears flopping madly. He stopped just short of her, and she reminded herself it was love of Benjamin that had convinced her aunt to go to the hospital.

"You saved her life, Porky," she whispered to him, then glanced around to make sure Rand had not heard her.

The pig looked at her. He seemed to have a grin on his homely face. *She saved mine, too.*

Chelsea laughed. She was reading things into his

bright, beady little eyes. "I'm exhausted," she said out loud. She really was. She'd had that cell phone in her hot little hand, and the only person she'd called was her father! That was not how a rational woman thought! She *should* have called Barry. Betsy. Lindsay. The list of who she could have and should have called was endless.

"I can look after the chickens if you're tired," Rand said. He was beside her. He gave Benjamin an affectionate chuck under the chin and scratched the top of his head.

"I can't believe you touched him!"

"He actually feels nice," Rand told Chelsea.

"Nice, how?" she demanded.

"Clean. His skin is soft and silky."

Okay, now she was faintly jealous of the pig. "And you thought I'd led a sheltered life," she muttered, shaking her head.

He was so close to her that if she leaned over just a little bit her shoulder would touch his. Then he'd know what soft and silky were all about!

"I'm not that tired!" she said out loud, giving herself a mental shake.

Rand avoided her eyes. He moved a step away from her, as if he knew how close she was to brushing against him.

"Really," he said abruptly. "I can handle the chickens."

Oh, she knew that. She knew he could handle the chickens and the pig! But how would he handle a different kind of touch, silky and soft and lovely?

She was talking about temptation. Rand looked absolutely stunning right now, gazing down at the pig with affection, whiskers roughing his cheeks and his chin, his eyes dark with weariness. If he touched her, would they both be lost? Being this tired was just a little bit like having had a few drinks too many. It made her feel slightly bold, slightly edgy, slightly daring.

"I'm not that tired!" she repeated again.

He thought she was talking about helping with the chickens, or he pretended that he thought that. But she truly wasn't so tired or so weak or such a naive ninny that she was going to fall for her bodyguard, of all things. It would be like a bad movie.

So, Rand Peabody had redeemed himself slightly in her eyes, when he'd given her his cell phone, no questions asked. So what? That would be a damn poor excuse to fiddle with this undeniable current of awareness that was leaping in the air between them.

The man, she reminded herself sourly, had disposed of her cell phone, which was why she had needed to borrow his in the first place. Then he'd acted *surprised* that she had been able to get Hetta in the car and keep her calm. And to top it all off he'd decided *for her* how to treat poor little Candy in her ugly green uniform who had only wanted an autograph.

Chelsea wanted to run into that house, feast on the leftover meat pies, have a shower and go to bed. She wanted to be away from him and the green of his eyes and the sensuous curve of his lips and the unconscious tautness of the muscle in his forearm that bunched and unbunched as he stroked the pig. But if she ran away, there was a chance that he'd *know* she was running from how attracted she was to him. He looked like he was the kind of man who already knew such things, so she had some backtracking to do.

"*You* can help *me* with the chickens," she said in a princess to peasant voice that would annihilate any indication she had ever given that she might want to be touched by him.

He flinched, caught the reaction, then shrugged with total indifference. He let her lead the way to the chicken coop. She resisted the urge to cover her nose. He folded his arms over his chest and regarded her, waiting for orders.

"I guess they need some food," she said, trying not to sound tentative. "You do that."

"Yes, ma'am."

She stuck out her tongue at his back as he moved away from her, but then watched mesmerized as he reached up a shelf, yanked down a fifty pound sack and tossed it over his shoulder.

How on earth did her aunt do that by herself?

Unfortunately Chelsea *liked* watching him work— the easy play of muscle, the poetry of masculine strength—and that was not the point of this exercise.

He turned, caught her staring, lifted a brow.

"Um, I'm just going to—"

"—collect eggs?" he suggested silkily.

"Exactly!" If she tried to retrieve one of those sacks, she would probably end up underneath it, her limbs flailing unattractively.

She soon realized his suggestion was a trap. The chickens were none too willing to surrender their eggs. They flapped their wings; they refused to budge off their nests. The eggs she did manage to wrestle away from the hens were streaked with chicken poop. It was making her feel quite light-headed, until an annoyed hen pecked her finger. She stifled a scream when she saw blood coming out of her knuckle.

She hadn't stifled it enough. Rand was at her side in an instant. She stuck her hand behind her back. He drew it out and looked at it. If he thought her hand was soft and silky and lovely to touch he refrained from mentioning it.

He let it drop back to her side. "I'll put some antiseptic on it when we get to the house," he said.

As if she was letting him touch her again! "It's nothing."

"You don't want to leave a cut that you pick up in a place like this unattended."

"Then I can clean it myself, thank you," she said stiffly.

"Why don't you go do that, and I'll finish up here?" He sounded weary, as if she was just a big nuisance instead of any kind of help at all!

"I'll finish what I'm doing!" she said. She hoped he would have the good grace to chase the remaining chickens from their nests, but he did not. He gave her an exasperated look and went back to what he was doing.

So, she gathered eggs, shooed chickens, gagged, gave little startled shrieks when the more aggressive hens cackled or flapped their wings at her and gathered more eggs. Rand seemed oblivious to her as he shoveled and carried huge sacks of feed and pails of water.

He was oblivious to her, while she was torturously aware of every twitch of his fabulous muscles. She passed close to him and was aware, acutely, of the sweet tang of his sweat.

They had turned on the radio—Rand remembered her aunt said the chickens liked it—and soon Betsy Blinkoff came on again with the very same story Chelsea had heard this morning. She glanced his way. If he listened to the story he gave no indication. He just kept working, the smooth play of masculine strength bent to the task at hand.

Finally they were done. He took the huge basket of eggs from her, and she was too tired to protest.

"You go shower," he said, when they reached the house. "I'll fix something for supper."

"I'm too tired to shower."

"Yeah, well, you stink. And don't forget to put antiseptic on your finger."

"I stink?" she sputtered.

"Yes, *amiira*, you stink."

"What does *amiira* mean?"

"Princess."

It didn't sound like an endearment, either. "Have you been in the military?"

"What would make you ask that?"

"You have a certain tone I don't like."

"Hey, I'm tired, I'm dirty and I'm at the end of my patience." He pointed at the stairs. "This is not open for discussion. Go. Shower. You're ruining my appetite."

"If I refuse?"

"I'll throw you in there myself."

Her mouth worked soundlessly, indignantly. She debated slapping him. Instead she dissolved into giggles. She couldn't help it. She, Chelsea King, smelled so bad she was ruining somebody's appetite? Somebody so handsome that she didn't want to be ruining his appetite in any way!

She gave him a mock salute and clicked her heels. "Yessir."

"That's better." He chose to ignore the sarcasm. He actually grinned at her, a grin so authentic and boyish it made her heart stand still and she found herself right back at the place she had tried so hard to outrun. She scurried by him to the shower.

"Whoo-eee," he said as she went by him. He waved at the air in front of his nose. She had fought the urge to slap him but now she punched him—hard—on the shoulder and dissolved into giggles again when he grabbed his injured part and crossed his eyes in pretended agony.

Still, she had to admit he'd been right about the necessity of the shower. The stinging needles of hot water brought her back to her senses somewhat. She applied some iodine to her chicken-bitten finger, then went into her bedroom wrapped in a towel and found clean jeans and a T-shirt. She was not back to her senses enough to figure out something more alluring to wear!

She knew what she *should* do was get down that file she had hidden in the back of her closet and have a look at it while he was busy doing other things. But she didn't. In bare feet, her hair wrapped in a towel, she went back down to the kitchen. Pathetic as it was, she wanted to be in the same room with him—not that he was going to know that!

He was talking on the phone, and he stopped what he was saying abruptly when she entered the room.

Had he been talking about her? He covered the receiver with his hand.

"Could you make a salad?"

Well, she doubted it. She thought she'd just refuse, but apparently whoever he was speaking to doubted her culinary abilities as well because Rand listened for a moment and then grinned that heart-melting grin.

"McPherson says he's betting next month's salary that you don't know how to make a salad," he said.

"Which McPherson? My brother-in-law or my brother-in-law's brother?"

"Cameron."

"Oh, goodie, the one I can have fired." She opened the fridge. In a drawer in the bottom she found lettuce, tomatoes and celery. How hard could it be to make a salad? Something in the oven smelled good, so Rand had done his part.

"She says she's having you fired," Rand reported. "Don't lose any sleep over it. It's her favorite threat."

"Quit laughing at my expense," she said, turning back to the counter laden with things that might be good in a salad.

"Or you'll have us fired?" Rand cracked up. His laughter was intoxicating—deep and rich and melodious. So was the twinkle in his eye.

It was still at her expense.

She waltzed over to him. "Stop laughing at my expense, or I'll…"

His eyes glittered with amusement. "You'll what, *amiira*?"

"…kiss you."

The laughter died abruptly. He stared at her. His gaze, not the least amused, drifted to her lips. "Cam, I've got to go." He hung up the phone and folded his arms across his chest.

"Don't make threats you aren't prepared to carry through with," he said softly.

Her heart was hammering very fast, but she kept

her tone light. "What makes you think I won't carry through?"

He dropped his arms and took a step toward her. She took a hasty step back and dropped a tomato on the floor.

"That," he growled.

Underneath the cool polish of his reserve, she had the feeling he really did feel *threatened*. She recognized a startling truth. He found her attractive. That was nothing new. Men always found her attractive. What was new was that he was fighting it. Instead of begging her for one little kiss, one little glance, one little touch, he was putting up walls higher than she could scale.

"I wouldn't kiss you right now, anyway," she said breezily, bending and retrieving the tomato. "You smell like a chicken."

"Let's get something straight," he said, "You're not kissing me, ever."

She turned back and looked at him narrowly. So, he was still in his bossy, military mode, was he?

"Ever is a long, long time, Mr. Peabody," she said huskily. Her attention drifted to his lips. They were frowning, and it didn't disguise how full and sensuous they were. It had started as a game, but suddenly she really did want to taste him. She wanted it as badly as she had ever wanted anything in her life, and the power of the desire shocked her.

"I'm not your latest toy, Miss King," he said coldly, and she was humiliated to think her thoughts had telegraphed so clearly across her face. "Don't think you can play with me. I'm going to shower now."

"Call me if you need your back washed," she

retorted, and he gave her a look so smoldering it nearly scorched her.

"Don't play with fire."

But she could tell by the red-hot feeling that was tingling through her that she already was playing with fire.

"I made my terms clear," she said. "Don't laugh at my expense, and your lips…and your back…are perfectly safe."

He glared at her. "Forgive me, *amiira*, I forgot my place. I thought I was teasing you, but I guess I was laughing at your expense. A thousand pardons."

And then he was gone.

"Maybe I was just teasing, too!" she shouted after him, but the only response she got was the slamming of the bathroom door upstairs.

Chelsea was aware she was shaking. How had it ended like that?

She had never been good at chemistry, but she knew that was what was in the air between them. And that chemistry was a delicate thing. Something could go from being benign to explosive with just a hint of imbalance.

He was absolutely right about one thing.

She shouldn't play with fire.

Maybe he was right about two things, actually, though the second was harder to admit. Maybe she did have a bit of a princess—*amiira*—attitude. Maybe she did have a tendency to make everything about her. Maybe she did have a tendency to take things too seriously, to take offense too quickly.

She thought this morning, how setting Betsy Blinkoff straight had been her biggest concern. Now that seemed ridiculously small, and all about *her,* as if there weren't more important things in the world than addressing ridiculous rumors and gossip.

"I hate introspection," she reminded herself. "It gives me a headache."

As for infatuation, she was never contemplating that word again!

When Rand stripped down and got in the shower he discovered Chelsea had used almost all the hot water. Of course, it would never occur to the princess that there was a limited supply of anything, or that there was anything on the face of this earth that she could not have.

That might not bode well for him, given the wanting he had seen in her eyes.

His shower was luke warm and then cold, and he found himself glad for it. It cooled his temper, not to mention other things that had been raging white-hot and nearly out of control since she had tried to manipulate him with her lips.

"Touchy," he berated himself. He was being way too touchy. Of course, he had never wanted anything more in his whole life than to cross that small distance between them and kiss her senseless.

He cursed himself softly. He was tired. And Cameron had not given him good news.

The ongoing investigation had turned up a very likely suspect. Cameron's team was almost certain they had traced the letters to a grounds maintenance man at her California condo. The man, Burton Jones, had been scheduled to work at four this afternoon and had been a no show. He lived with his mother, and she didn't know where he was, either. She said he left for work at three, the same as always. Which at least meant he wouldn't have had time to make his way to Virginia. Cameron said they were watching for him at the O'Hare clinic, since that was where rumor had placed Chelsea.

Maybe that was why he'd gone off the handle about the kiss thing. He was worried about her. She'd probably been nice to that guy, the same way she had planned to be nice to the lady at the hospital. Maybe she'd made teasing remarks about kissing Burton, too. Maybe she'd tried out some of her amazing feminine allure, unaware of how much power she wielded, how the wrong person wouldn't back down.

Her using her lips as a weapon—or merely threatening to—was enough to make the most stable of men feel a moment's insanity, as Rand had just learned up close and personal! What he had wanted to do when she waltzed into the kitchen barefoot and smelling of soap was grill her about the grounds guy until he had bullied every single encounter and every exchanged remark—however casual—out of her. He sighed. According to Cameron, Jacob King was still adamant that she not know she was in danger. He wanted her protected in every way; her emotional health guarded as strenuously as her physical.

"We just don't let her know what's going on," Cameron said. "I mean the stalker is only part of this week's list of weirdos. Some young guy in Ohio is trying to book her for his senior prom next spring, the magazine *Muse* is willing to pay a million dollars for a nude shot of her and some creep claims he got his hands on a few strands of her hair, ran DNA on it, and he's really her long, lost cousin."

Rand tried to decide which of the three he'd like to kill first. Make that four, counting the stalker. Was he any better than any of those people? How could he claim to be, when simply looking at her lips made him think lecherous thoughts! He was pretty sure making her protection his first priority would not include being coerced into fighting with her, no excuses about how tired he was!

He got out of the cold water and wrapped a towel around himself. He opened the bathroom door a crack and listened. He could hear her smashing things around and cursing the tomatoes.

She had been thrust into a different world, and she had coped better than he could have imagined. Faced with the crisis with her aunt she had done magnificently. He needed to remember that. He dressed in clean jeans and a shirt.

Taking a deep breath, he went back down to the kitchen. Her *salad* was in a huge bowl in the middle of the table. The head of lettuce had been chopped into what appeared to be four equal sections. On top of that were severely traumatized tomatoes. It looked like she had tried to cut them with a wooden spoon. Whole celery stalks decorated the outer edges of the bowl.

She was at the sink, with her back to him.

He took a deep breath.

"Chelsea?"

She glanced back at him.

"I want to apologize," he said. "I shouldn't have talked to you like that."

She looked away, but not before he saw her blush.

"It's okay," she said, not turning around again. "We're both beyond tired, I'm sure."

"That doesn't make it okay. Not for me."

She turned and looked at him. She still had the towel wrapped around her head, but some hair had escaped and she blew a strand of shimmering silver out of her eye. "Okay, you're forgiven. Does that make you happy?"

"Yes, it does," he said, but he was aware it didn't. Not at all. There was only one thing that would make him happy.

And, as was the way of life, it was the one thing he couldn't have.

He took the reheated meat pie out of the oven, and she brought over whatever she had been washing in the kitchen sink. Radishes. She placed them in the salad bowl, on top of the tomatoes, whole.

While she attacked the meat pie, he tried to figure out the most diplomatic approach to the salad.

"So," he said, after a while, "you don't eat like someone who needs to go to an eating disorder clinic."

"I don't have an eating disorder!"

"Obvious. Does it bug you?"

She laughed. "It did this morning! But I feel as if I was a different person this morning."

He took a chunk of lettuce out of the bowl and contemplated it uncertainly. Aware she was watching him, he set it down on his plate and separated the leaves. A little garden dirt still clung.

"In what way were you a different person this morning?" he asked, and took a bite of his lettuce. It wasn't the first time he'd eaten things distinctly gritty.

"Well, there were way more important things to think about today. You know what I've been thinking?"

He chewed the lettuce slowly. "No. What?"

"I didn't want to come here. But my aunt might be

dead right now if you and I hadn't arrived yesterday. Don't you think that's amazing?"

He nodded, uncertain where she was going with this.

"Don't you think it's amazing how things sometimes fit together even when you don't think they're going to? Do you believe in a bigger plan?"

The question took him off guard, rattled him, like her question about prayers earlier. He was a man whose faith, as humble as his version of that had been, had been shattered as surely as his face all those months ago.

Sometimes things fit together even when you don't think they're going to. Like him and her? It was a combination so unlikely it would seem only God himself could have come up with it.

But thankfully he was saved from answering.

She helped herself to some salad. She looked down at her lettuce and went very pale. She pushed back her chair, screamed. The chair toppled and she hit the floor.

He was picking her up and cradling her in his arms before he even knew what he was doing. "Are you okay?"

She nodded against his chest. "I think I scraped my elbow."

He turned her arm over. Her elbow did have an ugly red scrape on it. He did what he had sworn not to do.

He kissed her. He kissed the scrape on her elbow.

She held up her iodine dipped finger to him, and he kissed that, too. She seemed very pleased with that.

"There was a bug in the lettuce," she said, but her voice was faraway. She added, "Ugh," but it was a dreamy afterthought. She reached up and touched his lips with her fingertips.

The last thing he was thinking was "ugh."

He knew if they stayed like this, she was going to kiss him. It had been in the air between them—hinting, teasing, dancing, ducking—from the moment they had first met.

He knew he could not allow it to happen.

But a man could only be so strong....

"Don't worry about a little bug," he said. "I've eaten them as the main course."

There! That should just about do in any attraction she was feeling to his lips.

"Ugh!" she said, and she meant it this time.

He helped her off the floor, then let her go instantly. "Are you okay?"

She nodded. "I'm very tired."

Her lip trembled and he thought, *if she cries, I'm done*.

But she didn't cry. She blinked rapidly, and then announced, "I'm going to bed."

That was good. That was very good. He warned himself not to say anything that would delay her exit.

"Good night, then, *kariima*."

"What's that mean?"

Her exit delayed. "It's a variation of princess," he said, forcing himself to keep it short. That wasn't quite true. It meant noble, valuable, precious. All the things he did not want to admit she was becoming to him.

He watched her go up the stairs and straightened the kitchen. Then, he looked at the time and turned on the TV. There were two black and white channels, one of which was showing *Celebrity Today*. They just had word in: Chelsea King was not at the O'Hare Clinic.

He braced himself.

Chelsea King was in Farewell, Virginia. The announcement was accompanied by a grainy cell phone quality photo that showed him escorting Chelsea down the hospital steps. She must have turned back slightly, because the camera phone had caught her profile.

"We don't know who the new hot guy is, but we'll keep you posted. And for tonight, that's our show."

He shut off the TV. Damn, damn, damn.

He needed to look at that file with her name on it, but he was too tired, and just a little too aware that it seemed like an invasion of her privacy. That's what happened when a job got too personal.

Tonight, he was just going to have to make their location as secure as he could. He locked the doors, and as an extra security measure pulled the pig's mat in front of the back door. Benjamin stared sadly at his old spot for a few seconds, then glumly moved with his mat to the new location. Good. It would take a lot of noise to push by a four-hundred-pound Yorkshire pig. Then he moved the couch in front of the front door. The entrances were covered. He hit the sofa without even taking off his shirt and was sleeping in thirty seconds.

Chapter Six

Chelsea felt as if she had barely gone to sleep when she felt a touch on her shoulder.

"Sabah al-kheir," Rand said softly. "Good morning."

She opened her eyes, but felt as if she was still dreaming. Rand was crouched beside her bed. He made her think of a warrior, his strength a shield that made his presence in the sanctuary of her bedroom both formidable and reassuring. She wondered, in that vulnerable moment upon waking, before her own shields went up, what it would be like to be the woman who coaxed a smile from him, who found the tender heart barricaded behind all that power.

A renegade thought, right up there with kissing him. What would it be like to wake up beside this man? To feel not just his strength but his tenderness? To share his world and his experiences, which seemed wider and deeper and more colorful than her own? Foolish thoughts, but a person's heart was sometimes foolish— foolishly honest—in those moments before mind was fully awake.

Sleepily she replied, *"Sabah al-warada,"* and was rewarded when Rand looked both surprised and pleased. He reached out. For a moment she thought she would feel the hardness of his callused palm against the softness of her cheek, but he pulled back before he actually touched her. He stood and moved toward the door hastily, as if he too felt the pull of things between them.

"You're awake?"

She nodded.

"I already looked after the chickens," he said, "but if we're going to get the produce to the soup kitchen we need to get started."

"What time is it?"

He glanced at his watch. "Nearly seven."

Seven in the morning, and she, Chelsea King, was going to get up to pick potatoes. Not only that, she wanted to get up. She felt *eager* to get up, get going, *be* with him.

She reminded herself of his stern warning yesterday. That they were *never* going to kiss, that he was not her toy. But following on the heels of that, she remembered his apology, and how he *had* kissed her. Okay, not in the way she wanted to be kissed, but still he had kissed her elbow where she had scraped it and the tip of her chicken nipped finger. Really, he had broken the *kiss* vow within minutes of making it.

So, maybe Mr. Rand Peabody was not quite so formidably strong and stern as he wanted her to think he was.

So, maybe, she told herself, throwing back the covers

and leaping from the bed, *what you need to be doing is finding out if you* like *him.* Beyond the tantalizing pull of all things physical, did she like who he was?

She'd been given days with him to find out, and suddenly it seemed like such a gift—this strange sojourn she had been sent on. She'd been given the gift of being in the right place at the right time, so that her aunt could live. Maybe she was still in the right place at the right time. Maybe she, too, could live. Really live. A different life than the one she had chosen so far.

"So," she asked him, moments later as she sorted through her aunt's cereal selection, "What's the difference between *sabah al-warada* and *sabah al-kheir*?"

She sat across the table from him. He was dressed very casually today, in khaki shorts and a golf shirt. His legs were long and muscled and sun-kissed. He looked incredible, and the situation seemed *intimate*, the two of them alone together in the farmhouse, eating like a *couple*. He was even reading a newspaper as he sipped his coffee.

"Where did you get a newspaper?" she asked when it seemed like he planned to ignore her other question.

"It's delivered to the box at the end of the driveway. *Sabah* means morning," he said, a little too absently, not appreciating the nuances of the morning at all. "*Al-warada* means morning-of-roses—" did he blush ever-so-slightly, even though he didn't glance up from the paper? "—the second, morning-of-goodness. The usual response, to either would be *sabah an-nur,* morning of light."

"*Sabah an-nur,*" she repeated. It was before seven in the morning, and she was learning a foreign language in a small farm kitchen with an exotically dangerous man! Really, life could take you places you never expected it to go. Beautiful places, places of poetry.

"Where did you learn to speak Arabic?" she asked, determined to keep the conversation going.

"Jail," he answered. He didn't look up. It was a conversation killer if she'd ever heard one!

"Would you care to elaborate?"

He did look up then. "No," he said.

"Obviously my father did not hire an ex-convict to look after me," she said.

"I never said anything about being an ex-convict," he told her, then he got up and slapped her leg with the newspaper. "Ready to go?"

She followed him out to the garden, but if he knew she was looking daggers at the broadness of his back, he didn't let on. Benjamin followed on his heel like a loyal, if very large, dog. They all three stood and looked at the enormous garden.

"Do you know what a potato looks like?" she asked.

"Round? Brown?" he teased. "Sometimes red?"

"I meant the plant!"

"I know what you meant. I didn't want to admit I have no idea. I didn't grow up around such down-home things as gardens."

"What did you grow up around?" she asked while tentatively scraping the earth around a plant. "Do we need any beets?"

"Beets. I don't remember your aunt mentioning beets, but I think they'd be good in soup."

"Excellent," she said. "What did you say you grew up around?"

"I didn't say."

"Look, the air of mystery is wearing a little thin. You can tell me where you grew up. I promise I won't use it against you at a later date."

He tried not to smile and failed. "Okay, Miss Snoop. I grew up on military bases, some stateside, some foreign."

"I am not a snoop! I'm just being courteous. Showing an interest in you. What foreign bases?"

"Germany. Japan. England."

"So do you speak those languages, too?"

"As far as I know my English is passable."

She threw a little clod of dirt at him, he deftly stepped out of the way. "How many languages?"

He rolled his eyes, letting her know he had not changed his opinion of her as Miss Snoop. But he did answer. "Once you have bent your mind around learning one different language, you seem to pick up others fairly easily. I speak five languages fairly fluently and have a smattering in several others."

She wrestled a very large beet from the ground. There seemed to be an awfully lot to know about Mr. Peabody. She could spend a lifetime and not have all the answers she wanted. "Do you read and write different languages, too?"

"Marginally."

She sighed. Now there was a world that was closed to her. She didn't even read and write English all that well. Obviously he was smart and she wasn't—a major obstacle to romance.

Romance? Was she seriously contemplating such a thing with him?

A shiver went up and down her spine, when she realized she *seriously* was.

"I found the potatoes," he said.

He would *never* have anything to do with it. But, on the other hand, he'd said he would *never* kiss her, either.

Hey, way too fast, she told herself. She didn't even know him yet. She didn't even know if she liked him, beyond this feeling of having a sort of silly schoolgirl crush on a man who had obviously experienced things far outside her world.

Maybe that was all that made him intriguing. He was different. Unique. Strong in a way she had not experienced before. Being around him made her feel deliciously feminine, even without makeup on, even without a designer dress, even without the cameras flashing in her face.

She went to where he stood. He put his shovel in the soil and dug, and the heap of dirt produced potatoes! Ridiculous to think of it as some kind of miracle, but she got down on her knees and began to dig the potatoes out of the loosened dirt with her hands.

He joined her. There were big potatoes and small ones, and some so oddly shaped they both had to laugh when they found them. Every time they thought the hill was done, one of them found another potato.

"It's kind of like being on a treasure hunt," she said, as he finally moved on to the next hill, and she brushed the dirt off her knees.

"Okay, now that's a surprise."

"What is?"

"Chelsea King thinking digging for potatoes is like finding treasure."

"Well, it is!"

He looked at her. "You know what life has taught me?"

"What?" She was holding her breath, liking the way he was seeing *her*, not a job, not a responsibility.

"That treasure is always where you least suspect you'll find it," he said softly, "and that the most priceless gifts are the simplest things. Sunshine touching your face, the notes of music on evening air, an unexpected smile."

She did smile at him, because finally his guard was down, completely. Finally he had showed her something of who he really was.

And it took her breath away.

"So what would be on your list of priceless gifts, Chelsea?" he asked, his voice quiet, his eyes intent on her face as he leaned his chin on top of the shovel and watched her. He wasn't just being polite, either.

"Digging spuds," she said, suddenly as afraid to show him who she really was as she had been eager to find out who he really was.

He didn't let her off the hook that easily. "What else would be on your list?"

Different things than what she would have said yesterday. "On the very top of my list," she said, "would be spending time with my sisters and my dad."

"All the things you've had—the jewelry, the trips, the riches—and you know what you just told me?"

"What?"

"Only one thing counts. Love."

"Well," she said, suddenly terribly uncomfortable with *that* topic. "And Jimmy Choo shoes."

"Jimmy who?" He laughed, as she had hoped he would.

Side by side they dug the row of potatoes, until they had three baskets full of the little gems. They moved on to carrots. They chatted, less serious now, about music and movies and travels. They talked of childhood adventures and memories, of things that made them laugh. Suddenly, inexplicably, miraculously, it was easy being together. And wonderful.

When they finally had baskets full of onions, carrots, potatoes and beets, he looked at his watch. "If we're going to be there in time for this stuff to become soup, I think we'd better go."

"I wish we didn't have to," she said, wistfully. How she would have liked to hang onto this simple, sun-filled morning.

"Why? You aren't scared of rolling up your sleeves and making a little soup are you?"

"Soup for fifty people is not a *little* soup. It's not that, anyway."

"What is it then?"

"It just felt good to be out here, a million miles from the nearest place where anyone could recognize me. If they start asking for autographs at the soup place, it'll be wrecked."

"I agree. You're going to have a lot more fun at the soup kitchen if no one knows who you are."

"That's true." She held up her hands. They were filthy, dirt caked under broken nails. "Though this should convince anyone who's looking that closely."

"A few other small changes, and you'll look like someone else."

It was fun—and she could see he was a bit of an expert at this type of thing. He found a pair of her aunt's coveralls. She tucked her hair up under a ball cap, and he suggested she darken her brows with a bit of eyeliner.

"That looks ghastly," she said presenting herself to him a few minutes later. "One step from unibrow."

"And three million steps from Chelsea King."

"Should I draw a scar on my face, too?"

"No, but we could black out a tooth. That would be fun."

And suddenly it was fun, and she was laughing with him as they moved the baskets of produce from the garden to the trunk of the car. Rand had already told Hetta's loyal neighbor he would not be needed this morning.

Rand drove the car to town, not daring to look at Chelsea. Not daring because he was afraid he would be dazzled by her. Just as he had been, in the garden, watching her on her knees, digging potatoes, unmindful that she had a smear of dirt on her cheek. She had looked as beautiful as he had ever seen her look— wholesome and real.

Now she was sitting beside him in a pair of too-large overalls, a baseball cap pulled over her penciled brow. And she still looked gorgeous, still radiated *something*—a joy for life, an innocent wonder that left him flabbergasted and off balance.

As they drove into Farewell, Rand noted that several camera-laden people wandering the streets, undoubtably the paparazzi following up yesterday's "sighting." He was glad for the disguise—and for the part of town they headed to.

No one would look for Chelsea King here, in this section of town where some of the buildings had boarded up windows and papers blew down the streets and a glance down dark alleys showed the scurrying of feral cats.

"Are we safe here?" Chelsea asked in a small voice.

"That's my job," he reminded her, "to keep you safe. Don't worry about a thing."

He found the address he was looking for and pulled over underneath a large worn sign that said Bounty Kitchen. There was a scraggly line of people lined up outside the door and down the street.

"What are they doing?" she asked.

"I imagine waiting for lunch."

She was silent. When he came around and opened her door, she pulled her cap over her eyes, avoided looking at that line of desperate people in their worn clothes, avoided the expressions on their faces—flat, hostile, despairing.

He popped the trunk and handed her a basket. Several people materialized from the line and offered to help carry things in. Inside, the kitchen was cheerful and busy and Rand found himself thankful for that, for Chelsea's sake. A robust man greeted them like family when he found out Hetta had sent them. His face fell when he found out she was ill, but he recovered and put them to work.

"If you could peel the potatoes at that sink there."

Rand moved the huge basket of potatoes.

"Do you know how to peel potatoes?" Chelsea whispered.

"Oh, boy, do I know how to peel potatoes."

She laughed. "I thought that was only in the movies."

"Yeah. Think again."

Together they scrubbed the dirt from the potatoes,

peeled them, halved and then quartered them for the soup pot. An easy camaraderie sprang up between them again. When the potatoes were cooking, they were given other jobs—set tables, set out huge bottles of hand sanitizer at the front door. Serve soup.

Rand watched as Chelsea's original awkwardness disappeared. She greeted people, doled out soup and buns and greetings.

When the last of the line had gone by, they were encouraged to take their own soup and join the men and women at the tables.

"It's so quiet," she said. "Why isn't anybody talking?"

"Because they're hungry," Rand told her and did not miss her shocked look that people could be that hungry.

After they took their place a young man sat across from them, his jeans torn, his shirt faded almost transparent. He finished several bowls of soup before he seemed to notice them.

Rand introduced himself and Chelsea, first names only, and took the lad's hand. There was strength in that handshake. He said his name was Brody. He'd never done well in school, never learned to read properly, had found work in a mine for a while but then it had closed. He did lawns for people in the summer, whatever he could find. Did they know of any work he could do? He'd do anything.

Rand glanced at Chelsea. She was very pale. She looked like she was going to cry. This was just a little too much culture shock for her.

"Give me a number where I can reach you," Rand said. "I'll keep my ear to the ground for you."

Brody had no paper or pen, Rand had both.

"This is my cousin's number," Brody said. "He usually knows where to reach me. Anything you can find, sir. I appreciate it."

Rand nodded and looked again at Chelsea. Time to go. He got up and held Chelsea's chair for her. She actually stumbled on her way to the door. He got her into the car, but she wouldn't look at him, her face turned to the window.

"Brody was homeless, wasn't he?"

Her voice was a little squeak.

"So it would appear."

"Can you help him?"

"I don't know."

"It's because he can't read," she said.

"That's probably part of it."

Then she was sobbing helplessly, and Rand had no choice. He pulled the car over on the side of the road, heedless of the fact that he was on Main Street. He gathered her in his arms. Her cap flipped off and that silvery hair spilled out across his chest.

He allowed himself to touch it. He said softly, amazed at his own capacity for compassion,

"Hey," he said. "You can't take on the whole world."

Then, the flash of a camera alerted him to the fact that this was about the furthest thing on earth from a private moment.

Sarah Jane McKenzie shot a furtive look over her shoulder. It was two o'clock in the morning and the streets of Hollow Gap were rain-washed, dark and empty. She hated walking by herself at night, and she wished she'd called a cab.

But she had been, as always, ever-mindful of money. She was only a block from her apartment and she broke into a trot. She noticed a car parked across from her building, only because it did not fit in. No one in this neighborhood owned a Mercedes. The drug dealers went for the flashier models, the low slung sports cars.

She fit her key in the front door and fell inside. She stood with her back against it, panting. She wished she hadn't seen the car. It reminded her of the world she'd left behind. Of course, those reminders seemed to be everywhere. She went up the stairs, exhausted, unlocked her door and stepped inside her own small apartment.

And froze in the darkness.

Her apartment held a new aroma. One she would know anywhere. Of spice, of high wild places, the smell of a man. With her heart beating even harder than it had when she'd run that last block home, she reached for the light switch.

The overhead light came on. Just yesterday it had given her such pleasure to cover the bare bulb with a fixture. Today, all she could see was that Cameron McPherson was fast asleep on her couch. That car outside should have warned her!

He woke with a start, and she might have bolted back out the door, except for one small thing. When he awoke, and saw her, he smiled. A sweet, groggy smile that said things that weakened her: he had missed her and worried about her; he cared about her and was glad to see her. He sat up on the couch and stretched. Something fell off his lap onto the floor.

She folded her arms over her chest and tapped her foot to hide the furious beating of her heart, to hide how horribly vulnerable she felt. She tried not to think how she must look in her faded pink uniform with a white collar and a stained apron, her name tag crooked over her breast.

"What are you doing in here?" she demanded. "You can't just come and set up shop in a person's apartment!"

He shrugged. "Your landlord let me in."

Oh, yeah, her landlord would have practically been bowing to the expense of that suit, the authority of that handsome, clean cut face.

"How did you find me?" she whispered.

"You called from that phone booth on the corner."

"That was only a few days ago!"

"I'm good at what I do. I found the booth, then started asking questions, showing a picture of you."

"You don't have a picture of me!"

"There was one from Brandy and Clint's wedding. Do you want to see it?"

"No." But she found herself moving toward him, toward the picture he held out. She snatched it from him without touching his hand. If she touched his hand, or looked in his eyes, she knew she was going to be lost.

Though she didn't know exactly what that meant.

The picture was of her and Jacob King. Sarah was in an absolutely stunning designer dress that Chelsea had tried to give her, that Sarah had accepted, reluctantly, as a loan for the wedding. Another painful reminder of the life she had left behind. Dresses that dazzled and whispered and sang of the soft sensuality of a woman.

"That's what I didn't get," Cameron said slowly, taking the picture from her and gazing at it intently. "Chelsea told me she'd wanted to give you that dress and that you wouldn't take it. Too much money. So why would you refuse a dress worth who knows how much but then steal trinkets from Jake's office?"

She backed away from him, allowed her eyes to slide to the door.

"Those people don't have trinkets, they have heirlooms. Is that why you came?" she asked harshly. "To arrest me for stealing?"

His face went very cold. "You know that's not why I'm here."

"Then why couldn't you just leave me alone?"

"I came for the truth. I couldn't rest until I'd found out the truth."

"Well, go find it then, if you're so fired up good at your job."

"Here's the thing, Sarah. I think I already did. I think it's been staring me in the face the whole time. The truth is in that photo, isn't it?"

She looked back at the photo, and she felt like crying, at her face as she looked at Jake. At her grandfather. She looked radiant, as if she had discovered the oldest secret in the world. And perhaps she had. Family was everything. And she had wrecked it, walked away from it.

It was then that she noticed the book that had slid off his lap onto the floor. It was her grandmother's diary. She began to tremble.

. He noticed the direction of her gaze, picked the book up from the floor. "As soon as I walked in here," he said, "I was drawn to this. You had it set up on the shelf, as if it was some kind of shrine, as if it was the only thing you have any value."

It was. It was the record of who she really was and where she had come from.

"You look just like him," Cameron said softly. "I don't know why I didn't see it before. Other people did. Everyone kept remarking how much you looked like Brandy."

She did not cry, dammit, and yet the tears were slithering down her cheeks. This was the thing about family. It would require things of her she had never required of herself. It would require all her love and all her loyalty, all her honesty and all her ability to forgive.

Maybe that was the real reason why she had left, the real reason she had never told Jake the truth.

She slid another look at the door.

"You can go if you want, Sarah," he said softly. "I won't try to stop you. But I'd rather you did something else."

She looked, finally, into his eyes. They were warm with tenderness and strength. They were beautiful and real. Truth lived in his eyes.

"Let me take you home," Cameron McPherson said softly. "Sarah, let me take you home."

Chapter Seven

Rand disengaged himself from Chelsea and gave the photographer leaning over the hood of the car a mean look and a middle finger. The photographer was not easily intimidated and kept clicking away with his camera. Rand, who could always count on himself to be supremely cool under pressure, was shocked at the strength of his urge to get out of the car and pummel the man. Couldn't any fool see this was a bad moment for Chelsea?

She was more accustomed to intrusions into her private moments, and Chelsea crammed the hat back over her head and pulled it low. Rand slammed the car into gear and pulled away from the curb. His urge to squeal tires was not realized because he actually had to nudge the photographer with the car to make good the escape. He watched in the rearview mirror as the photographer scrambled toward his own vehicle.

"Hang onto your hat," he told Chelsea grimly, as he gunned the car. They were around the first corner before the photographer had even gotten his door open. Rand randomly took the next right and a left after that.

"I'm going to be in the paper looking like this," Chelsea said, but her heart wasn't in the complaint. "I don't even know how he knew it was me."

As if anyone else in the world, no matter how hard they tried, could imitate the glory of the hair that had sprung free, briefly, from her ball cap.

Rand shot her a look. She was obviously upset, and not about the photographer, either. Something had happened in the Bounty Kitchen while they listened to Brody. But the task at hand was to get out of town without being followed. Ten minutes later, watching the rearview mirror as much as the road in front of them, he was sure he had succeeded. He headed for the road that led to Hetta's farm.

But Chelsea sat like a stone in the front seat, hugging herself.

"What was it about that kid that upset you?" he asked. What had he missed?

"Nothing."

"Did I do something?"

"No." When they reached the farm, she charged out of the car and ran up the walk into the house. She ignored poor Benjamin Franklin, who looked almost human in his dejection.

Rand realized he'd left the door unlocked this morning.

He contemplated that, and the fact that he'd let his guard down enough in town that the photographer had been right on top of them before Rand had even noticed his approach. It was the kind of mistake that, in some of his former endeavors, could have left people dead. That could have been the result just now, too, had the person who approached the vehicle been the person stalking Chelsea, rather than a photographer.

Rand was shaken by these lapses. He was getting personally involved, acting like a spellbound schoolboy instead of like the absolute professional that he was. Chelsea King, with those big eyes and that hair and that smile, was wrecking his edge without half trying. He had to pull himself together, *right now*.

It was much too easy to believe, working by her side in the garden, peeling potatoes at the sink, looking into the amazing green-gold of those eyes, that the world was a good place, wholesome and fun and without danger.

Yet those eyes were creating a danger of their very own.

A danger to him.

He'd been lulled into a false sense of security. With that failure in mind, Rand went into the house just in time to hear her bedroom door slamming upstairs. He did a quick check of the premises, including the basement. The pig dogged his heels.

"Benjamin," he said, "you are a great watch pig. No one's getting into this place past you, are they?" Nothing in the house was out of place and he patted the pig on the head.

But even that comment, lighthearted, reminded him there was nothing lighthearted about what he was supposed to be doing. He needed to get on the phone and find out what progress had been made today. Had Jones been located? Had they confirmed the stalker was the maintenance man? He wanted to rip who ever had sent those letters limb from limb, which was not exactly a *professional* reaction, either.

Once he'd made some phone calls, he would read that file he'd been given about Chelsea. Both of those would be *professional* things to do.

He thought of her tears in the car, hot and puddling against his chest, the stricken look on her face as she had listened to the story of that young homeless man. He'd have to be heartless to leave her alone to deal with whatever she was dealing with.

"You are heartless," he reminded himself. But it didn't ring true, and despite his resolve to do otherwise, he went up the stairs two at a time and knocked on the door.

"I want to be alone."

There. It didn't get any clearer than that. Only it sounded like she was crying again. He knocked on the door a little harder.

"Go away!"

"Come on, Chelsea, I just want to talk for a minute."

No answer this time, so he opened the door. She was lying on her stomach on the bed, scrubbing furiously at a tear-streaked face as if she could erase the evidence that she'd been crying. All she'd done was rearrange her penciled brow so it was streaking down the bridge of her nose. Though no expert on sensitivity, even he knew it might be better not to mention that. He sat on the edge of the bed.

"What's this about?" he asked quietly.

"I'm having a moment," she said.

An understatement, but again he knew better than to

call her on it. "What was it about that kid that brought on this, er, moment?"

"It's not about him! It's about being stuck on this farm and not being at the wrap party for *The Third Entity* and the whole world thinking I'm in an eating disorder clinic."

"That's a lie."

"Oh! How would you know?"

"I played poker with you."

"Damn."

"Is it so hard to tell the truth?"

"Oh, look who's talking, Mr. I've-Eaten-Bugs-In-Jail-Card-Cheat. Sure, you want me to tell you everything about me, but you won't say a word about yourself."

He contemplated that for a minute. With tear streaks on her face, he saw something in her that was so lonely, despite the whirlwind life she led.

What could he do? He heard himself say, quietly. "What would you like to know?"

"Everything," she shot back. She sat up and folded her arms across her chest, waiting.

He heard stubbornness in her voice. And surrender in his own. "Okay."

"Well, maybe not everything," she said, with the faintest edge of panic.

Chelsea King was nowhere near being the sophisticated young woman she wanted the world to believe she was.

"I'll edit the X-rated scenes," he said dryly.

Her eyes went very wide.

"I was kidding." And he found himself telling her

things he had not expected he would ever tell anyone. He told her about growing up in a whole lot of different places, in different parts of the world. He talked about new schools and becoming increasingly wary of forming attachments. He told her how hard each move had been on his mother and how she had finally left.

He told Chelsea about how he felt the lesson he had learned from his father was *duty was everything* and the lesson he had learned from his mother was *never trust anything as nebulous as love.* Who would have thought she would be such a good listener, her head cradled in her hands, her luminous, expressive gaze locked on his face?

He told her how he had followed in his father's footsteps and joined the military and he told her about being singled out because of his gift for languages. He told her about his life in a secretive intelligence organization, a life that had become nomadic and shadowy, a life that didn't allow him to let other people in.

"A good fit," he said, "because I was lousy at letting other people in, anyway."

And then he told her about the last assignment— infiltrating a desert village on the other side of the globe that was said to be a terrorist stronghold. He'd claimed to be a teacher with an aid organization. He told her about falling in love with a gentle people and an ancient culture, and feeling torn about the double life he was living.

"I found myself. I felt I belonged somewhere and was needed. I loved teaching. Those people were so anxious to learn and they wanted only what every other person wants—better lives for their children. I would count those days as among the happiest of my life."

He was silent for a long time, remembering, and he was grateful that Chelsea did not push him.

Finally he continued. "It was almost a relief to come under suspicion."

He'd been thrown in jail, and he'd spent eight months there without the benefit of a trial, which may have been a good thing given the severity of sentences in that part of the world.

"The irony is that, again, I got to know people in a way I don't think I've ever known people. My cell mate had a different skin color, his religion was different, his mother tongue was different. And for all those differences, Rafik was the closest thing to a brother I had ever had. Maybe the closest thing to a family I had ever had. We watched out for each other. We watched each other's backs. Somehow, in that place that defied a man to laugh, we found laughter. We survived because of each other."

He was silent again for a long time, and, again, to his relief she did not push him, she just sat quietly, watching, waiting.

"I was broken out of that jail, a wall destroyed with explosives, a special task force sent in to get me. I nearly didn't make it." He touched his scars. "I learned later that Rafik didn't make it."

The silence folded around him. Then her hand touched his shoulder.

"Rand, I'm so very sorry."

It was not pity in her voice, but something entirely different. In a few very short days, something impossible had happened. He had let another person get close enough to him to care. It was written in the huskiness of her voice.

It was what was making this job impossible. Maybe the work he had always done was going to be impossible for him now. His bond with Rafik had given him his soul. Once a man found that, could he ever go back to what he had been before?

Or maybe Rafik had given him only half of his soul. Because looking at Chelsea, he felt as if the other half resided in her eyes.

"And then you took this job," she guessed.

"Not right away. I was in pretty rough shape for a while, and not just physically. I was in a dark place that I can't describe to you, nor would I want to."

Her hand tightened reassuringly on his shoulder, her touch like cool water after a long sojourn in the desert.

"When Cam contacted me about this position, I said no. But when he persisted, I knew I was being thrown a lifeline, a way out of that dark place. I knew accepting would give me a semblance of order and force me back into today, instead of yesterday. I thought the job would be nice and light, something far removed from the world I had known."

"And?" she asked huskily.

"And, it has been as far from my world as I could ever get. But nice and light?" He snorted. "I did not know anything as soft as you existed."

He could feel them both holding their breaths. She had been touching his shoulder, and now she sat beside him on the edge of the bed and took his face between her hands. She traced the lines of those scars. "You are so beautiful to me."

He drew in a sharp breath. "How can you touch those scars and say something so absurd?"

"From the moment, I saw you, I never saw scars. I saw strength. Beauty of soul."

"Stop it, Chelsea."

"I don't want to." Her lips found his cheek, and feather-soft, she anointed him.

He took her wrists and put her gently away, but it took everything—everything—he had to refuse the invitation of her hands and her eyes and her lips.

"I can't let this go there," he said, his voice ragged. "You know I can't."

She looked at him solemnly, and then, finally, nodded. "I know. I guess you wouldn't be who you are if you did. But will you go everywhere else?"

"I don't know what you mean," he said, but he was pretty sure he did.

"It would be unethical for you to take advantage of this relationship in a physical way," she said softly. "I understand that."

"Good," he croaked.

"But will you go everywhere else? Will you laugh with me? And get to know me? And hear my secrets?"

"Chelsea—"

"If you say no, then you're fired."

"Are we back to this? You know if Donald Trump gets tired of reality television, you could—"

"Don't make light of this. I'm serious."

"I know," he said. "That's what scares me."

"Harrumph. You've never been scared of anything in your whole life, Rand Peabody."

"Except this," he said softly. *Except this:* feeling so

vulnerable, so open, so on fire for another person. So aware of how a misstep, or his characteristic insensitivity, could harm. He ordered himself to disengage, and found out his strength, finally, had failed him. Because instead of disengaging, he spoke.

"Tell me your secrets," he said. And he meant it. He wanted to hear. Wanted to know. "It was a trade. A secret for a secret. Give me something to take with me when I go, a piece of you that no one else has ever had."

Had she heard the part that was most important for her to hear? That he would go?

She made a sound in the back of her throat, animal with longing, her meaning and her intention clear.

"Not that part of you," he said quietly. Something more than that, more sacred, more soulful. He wanted to see her heart.

"Okay," she said, and she took a deep shaky breath. "You know that young man we had lunch with? Brody?"

He nodded.

"He was me. If my dad wasn't who he was, I would probably be exactly where that boy was—homeless, begging for food and jobs."

"What do you mean?"

"He said he could never learn to read. I have dyslexia. It's a learning disability."

"I know what it is," he said quietly.

"With a great deal of tutoring and special attention, I learned to read and write. But badly. I would never do either for pleasure. I couldn't even read out loud to my aunt. I would have stumbled over words like a five-year-old at kindergarten. If not for my family status, I would be just like Brody."

"Aw, Chelsea."

"Don't you dare feel sorry for me!"

"Why would I feel sorry for you?"

"Because I'm stupid. There. That's my biggest secret. I'm dumb." The tears were spilling again, and she covered her eyes with her hands.

He pried them free and took her shoulders, gently, between his hands. He made her look into his eyes so that she would see the truth of what he was about to say. "That is not your biggest secret, Chelsea, not even close."

"It's not?"

"Reading. Writing. That's something you can't do. Your biggest secret—even from yourself—is what you can do."

She looked like she was going to melt into him, as if she had waited her whole life to hear those words. He wanted to stay in this moment forever, to cherish it, to make it—and the feeling between them right now—his touchstone, that *thing* he would hang onto when he was gone.

Instead he got up abruptly. "I think it's time to go feed the chickens. Are you coming?"

Regret flicked across her face and through the tapestry of her eyes. She, too, wished they could keep this moment and make it last forever.

But she shrugged off the feeling, and smiled at him.

"Only if you promise to swear at them in Arabic," she said, and bounced off the bed. Even he, insensitive boor that he had a history of being, could see the new lightness in her, could see how that secret had weighed her down, and how releasing it had given her wings.

Had his own secrets done the same thing to him?

"I promise," he said, but he was aware he was promising something quite different than to amuse her by swearing at the chickens in Arabic. His promise was to uphold her honor and to protect her from everything. Including himself.

As he opened the door for her and she walked by him, he caught her fragrance and closed his eyes. He had expected, when he had revealed something of himself to Chelsea, that it would allow her to trust him with her own secrets. What he had not expected was to feel so healed himself. By the words finally spoken, but more, by her acceptance of them and of him.

Taking a deep breath he followed her into the sunshine. She tilted her head back as though she had never felt the sun touch her skin before.

And he tilted his head back exactly the same way.

Chelsea threw her head back to the sun and savored what she felt. She was free. For the first time in her entire life she had told the complete truth about herself. Telling that truth had freed her because of Rand's acceptance, his lack of judgment, his belief that her biggest secret had nothing at all to do with her *disabilities* and everything to do with her *abilities*.

Still, despite her newfound awareness that she had not even begun to discover who she was—had not even begun to discover what gifts she had to give—she was painfully aware of how her life could have been Brody's life. Or Burton's life.

Burton worked on the grounds at her condo complex in California and she'd always been friendly to him, feeling a certain kinship with him because he did not seem too bright. But in the last few weeks before she'd come to Virginia, she'd started avoiding him because he seemed always to be where she was, staring at her, wanting small favors: an autograph, a picture for his mom, a small souvenir of some sort for his little sister.

Now, she felt guilty about avoiding him. She'd even imagined she'd seen him at the soup kitchen. Of course that hadn't been him. But the man that looked something like him had been a reminder she needed to mend her fences when she got home.

She turned to look at Rand. Something had relaxed in his face, and some finely held tension was gone from his shoulders. His eyes, when they met hers, had lost the gravity that had always haunted them. His gaze was warm, tinged with a faint tenderness that made her want to sing and skip and jump. That made her want to reach out and wrap her arms around him, hold him and never let him go.

But that was against the rules.

"You know what I want to do after we're done with the chickens?" she asked him.

"I'm afraid to ask," he said dryly.

"I want to make a cake."

"You think I know how to make a cake?" he asked. "My masculinity is offended."

"No," she said. "I think you know how to *read* how to make a cake without getting everything mixed up. I tried to make a cake once, after I'd moved out of my father's house. It seemed like it would be a nice *normal* thing to do. I thought it would make my new condo smell nice."

"And?"

"I put in twelve eggs. Because the recipe said 1-2

eggs. And I cooked it at five hundred and thirty degrees because I transposed the numbers, something people like me do quite a bit."

"Ah. That explains the card game."

"Yes, it does," she said sadly.

"How did the cake turn out?"

"Can you guess?"

"Um, yeah. But I bet your condo smelled the way you wanted it to."

"Yes, it did. I toyed with marketing the fragrance, Scorched Cake, but I decided against it."

"Anything you decided to market would probably sell by the zillions."

"I know! But that is a heavy responsibility."

"Speaking of heavy responsibilities," he said, holding the door of the chicken coop open for her, "I fed them fifty pounds of feed this morning. Can you scientifically explain how they could have possibly manufactured one hundred and fifty pounds of poop?"

She laughed. It felt so delicious to laugh with him. Even when he handed her the shovel life seemed funny and fun and full of *possibility*.

Later, when they came in, the phone was ringing. Rand must have forgotten to disable the phone after his call to Cameron, and Chelsea was glad, because the person on the line was Hetta. Her surgery had been a complete success, and she claimed to feel better than she had felt in twenty years.

She asked about the food bank and about Benjamin— Chelsea even held the phone by Benjamin's ear and he oinked excitedly at the sound of his mistresses's voice.

"Aunt Hetta?"

"Yes, dear?"

She was going to say one thing, but her courage failed her and she said another. "Do you have a good cake recipe?"

"I never write things down, dear. It's all in my head. I'll tell it to you if you want and you can write it down."

Chelsea took a deep breath. "I don't write down things, either," she said. "Because I always get it wrong. And that's why I wouldn't read to you that night you asked. Because I'm terrible at reading."

There was a long silence. "Chelsea, you should know that the reason I asked you to read wasn't because I don't see that well."

"It wasn't?"

"I could never really learn to read, either. The letters got mixed up in my head. I had that book there because one of the neighbors dropped by from time to time to read to me. I told her I couldn't see, too. I've been so ashamed, my entire life."

"Me, too," Chelsea whispered.

"Well, well, well," Hetta said, and then abruptly, "put that outrageously attractive man on the phone. I'll give the recipe to him. Are you two young folks behaving yourselves?"

Chelsea giggled. "As if he would do anything but."

Her aunt sighed. "Too bad, that."

"I agree."

"Oh, well, put him on the phone and I'll give him the recipe. We'll make it Devil's Food and hope that it lowers his resistance to temptation."

"Aunt Hetta, you and I are going to be the best of friends."

Hetta snorted, but Chelsea knew she was pleased. She passed the phone to Rand. An hour later, the kitchen was thoroughly coated in chocolate cake batter. Who knew electric beaters could make a mess like that if you lifted them out of the batter without turning them off?

Benjamin had placed himself in charge of cleanup of the lower levels, and Chelsea and Rand were licking batter off spoons while the cake cooked in the oven.

"You are great in the kitchen," Chelsea told him.

It hung in the air between them that he might be great in other areas of the house, too, but neither of them said anything.

"So," Rand said. "I was great at what you wanted to do, now is it my turn?"

She knew it would be prudent to ask him what he had in mind, but she threw prudence to the wind. "Sure." She hoped it involved locking lips.

He grinned. "I want to see dawn come up tomorrow."

"Yuck."

"It gets better. From the top of that mountain." He pointed out the window at Hetta's wild backyard.

She sighed. "I guess if I bring chocolate cake to fortify me." She loved it. Tomorrow she was going to be on the top of a mountain at dawn, eating chocolate cake.

"I'll take a picture of you," he promised. "And send it to the tabs. It should dispel any myths about the eating disorder."

"My hero."

"I bet that isn't what you'll call me when we're going up the mountain in the dark."

"Ha. Put a slice of chocolate cake on a stick. I'll follow you anywhere."

And she did. The next morning, exhilarated, she stood at his side on what seemed to be the highest mountain in the world. No wonder her sister Brandy loved this kind of thing. No wonder Jessie wanted to live here when she got back from her honeymoon. No wonder her father had lifted his eyes to these mountains at Jessie's wedding and then looked at Chelsea, willing her to see what he saw.

Now she did.

They watched the sun break over the peaks of the mountains that surrounded them, its rays slowly painting the valley below—her aunt's farm and Farewell and everything in between—in gold.

"You know what, Rand?"

"Hmm?"

The deep contentment in his voice made her happy.

"I think you are going to help me see the world in a deeper and more meaningful way."

He laughed. "Whatever."

"No, I mean it."

She knew that he was finding her ability to have fun a good balance for his tendency to be too serious. She was teaching him to laugh. He was teaching her to think.

There was an irony in their growing respect and liking for one another, because on the surface they would have seemed like exact opposites. Rand might have seemed the most selfless of men, one who had devoted his whole life to service for his country. Honestly, she might have seemed like the most selfish of women, one devoted only to the superficial, to those situations that demanded nothing of her, that allowed her to keep her secrets hidden.

Yet, in her new wisdom, Chelsea was beginning to see they were not opposites. They had both used the roles they played to keep them from what they feared most—true intimacy, being accepted for what they really were. The roles had imprisoned them in a place of deep loneliness. Here on her aunt's farm they were learning to be free. Something exhilarating was in the air—discovery.

A precursor to love.

It came to her suddenly, as dawn turned the world gold, a whisper of intuition and of inspiration.

"I'm not hiding it anymore," she announced. "I am not going to try to hide the fact I have a handicap from the world. I'm going to talk about it. To shine a spotlight on it so that people give money to research and education. So that people like that boy we had lunch with can get help. So that nobody has to be ashamed again."

Rand turned his face from the sun.

"That's exactly what I meant," he said, and she could hear the pride and approval in his voice. "It's not about what you can't do. Your biggest secret, Chelsea, has always been about what you can do."

It felt as if she had never had a moment like this in her entire life, and she drank it into her heart and soul, having no idea she was going to need every bit of the strength of this moment to sustain her through what lie ahead.

Chapter Eight

Chelsea could not sleep. The house was quiet. She and Rand had finished playing poker an hour ago. She had laughed so hard her stomach still hurt. As she had undressed for bed, she had laughed again when she had found a card she had forgotten about stuffed down her shirt. She was not sure there had ever been a period in her life so filled with laughter, discovery and wonder, as the past few days had been.

How could she sleep when she was on fire with life and a newfound sense of purpose? She was on fire with the way it felt to be around Rand—how he made her laugh and think and made her so much *more* than she had ever been before.

Am I falling in love with him?

Of course she was! How could she not? Any red-blooded woman in her predicament would do the very same thing!

Yet it felt way more personal than that. Somewhere, somehow, her feelings were sliding out of that infatuation stage and into something deeper and brighter and more breathtaking. But the thought seemed so big and so dangerous and so exciting she could not even contemplate it, not if she ever hoped to sleep again! If she did think forbidden thoughts and contemplate strange and exotic new worlds, she might lose the grip she had on herself, that one shred of sanity that prevented her from crossing the narrow hall that separated her room from his.

She listened, heard his bedsprings creak, as if he, too, was restless. What did he wear to bed? Was he lying there, arms folded under his head, staring at the ceiling? Was he thinking of her? Was he smiling?

"Stop it!" Chelsea ordered herself.

With great effort, she forced her thoughts in a different direction. She decided her intention, quite simply, (besides to marry Rand someday and live happily ever after, not that she was letting her mind go *there*) was to be the most amazing spokesperson for learning disorders that had ever been. She was going to single-handedly shatter the remaining stigma attached to dyslexia and bring attitudes out of the darkness. More, Chelsea King was going to make sure that every man, woman and child in America understood dyslexia and the crippling personal and societal price being paid because of the lack of understanding of this disorder.

"So, there!" she said out loud.

But talk was cheap, ideas only had power if they were brought to fruition. She needed a *plan*, a *how* to go with her *why*.

The first thing she would do, to draw attention to her

cause, was use her celebrity for something useful. She would host a charity auction. She could ask her friends to give her things to auction off to the public: Jenn's poodle's diamond collar, one of Lindsay's famous handbags, some of her own designer clothes, maybe some props from Barry's movie.

"I need to write this down," she said out loud, aware of how ideas could fly at this time of night and be gone by morning.

She marveled at that. She was going to write something down—in defiance of a handicap that made her writing so bad. This was how it started—with one person saying *no more*. No more shame. No more secrets. No more silence.

"Good motto," she congratulated herself.

Still, Chelsea was so unaccustomed to this activity, she did not even possess a piece of blank paper. Hetta would have some somewhere, but just before she went out her bedroom door to search the house she remembered the file tucked away on her top shelf.

There would be papers in there that she could scratch notes on the back of. She reached into the closet, pulled down the file and opened it. Papers, just as she had guessed, and all deliciously blank on one side. She might not have even read that top letter, except that it had Rand's name on it, and it popped out at her as if it was blinking in neon.

It was correspondence from Cameron McPherson to Rand *begging* him to protect Chelsea. Protect her? Her brow furrowed, she read on.

At first she didn't quite get what she was reading. She hadn't received any threatening letters. Her life was not in danger. Then, sudden understanding hit her, and, with her hands trembling ever so slightly, she put aside Cameron's letter to Rand.

Underneath it were a stack of letters, indeed addressed to her, and so vile, malicious and angry that she felt her stomach turn as she tried to read each one.

"At least someone has worse writing skills than mine, ha-ha," she said, in an effort to quell the fear that crawled along her spine.

She hadn't opened her own mail in years. She simply got too many letters—gifts, pleas for money, photos from strangers, marriage proposals—to even begin to deal with them. Her correspondence and her bills were all rerouted to her father's office where everything was looked after seamlessly.

Still, despite the fact that the arrangement had always worked for her, Chelsea felt the insult of not being told the truth about why Rand Peabody had suddenly put in an appearance in her life, why her old bodyguard had disappeared without a proper goodbye, why she had been exiled to her aunt's farm. The whole thing had been handled as if she was a child. No, as if she was an *idiot*. Too stupid, to get it. She felt so angry at Rand.

Why hadn't he told her? If not at first, over the last few days as the trust and camaraderie had built between them? She would have said, even five minutes ago, that he was a man she could have trusted with her life. But what had he trusted her with?

He had not trusted her with the *truth*.

And wasn't the building block of all other trust?

Her rational mind tried to remind her of all the things he had trusted her with, *truths* about himself, but she shoved those thoughts aside. None of that mattered. She *wanted* to be angry. Rand had not trusted her with information about *herself*, about her life.

And maybe, in a way, she had brought this scenario down on herself. Really, would anything in her lifestyle over the past five years have encouraged anyone to see her as mature? Smart? Able to deal with this kind of crisis in a rational way?

No. She had played a role. She had been the princess. She had *wanted* to be seen as superficial, as the party girl, because that role was so damned easy. Even now, the role offered comfort, because she certainly didn't want to go discuss her discovery of this file with Rand in a mature, adult way. She wanted to go scream at him, rant at him, have a tantrum, make a scene.

What you want is not to love him so much that he can hurt you. What you want is to chase him away before that happens, a voice inside her head said. *This is your excuse.*

Chelsea took a deep breath and mulled over her options. A middle of the night scene felt as if it would be satisfying and safe—she could play the role of a rich spoiled girl in an absolute snit. But when she contemplated going back to that she could feel an emptiness inside her that she didn't like. She was not so sure she *could* go back, even if she wanted to.

Chelsea decided to do something different, to act as if she was that mature adult, instead of giving in to her childish impulses. She'd go downstairs and make a cup of cocoa. For once in her life she would think things through before she took a course of action.

Chelsea made her way quietly down the stairs and flipped on the light.

Benjamin blinked at her from his little mat by the door, yawned and then got up and stretched. He came over on his cute little split-toe pig feet and sat in front of her.

Tentatively she reached out and touched his head.

Rand had been right. His skin was as soft as silk. Benjamin grunted happily, squeezed his eyes joyously shut and preened under her fingers. For a long time, she stood, transfixed by the moment, acknowledging her own transformation. She had become a person who could see the beauty in a pig! Even after she had just received upsetting information.

The phone ringing jolted her out of her introspection, and she tried to grab it before it woke Rand. Had something happened to her aunt? To her father? To one of her sisters? It seemed the only news that ever arrived in the middle of the night was bad.

"Hello," she said tentatively.

"Hello, Chelsea?"

"Aunt Hetta, are you okay?"

"I'm fine, dear. The doctor told me today I should be home in a week. I'm sorry to call so late, I was wanting to talk to Rand."

Oh, sure, another person who was not quite going to treat her like an adult. What did her aunt need to talk to Rand about that she couldn't talk to her about?

"You can tell me," she said firmly.

Hesitation.

Then Rand's voice came on the line, sleepy, as if he had not been troubled by restlessness at all. "Hello?"

"Hello, Rand, Hetta King here." She sounded very relieved. "Chelsea, would you mind hanging up?"

As a matter of fact, yes, she would mind hanging up.

So, she wasn't going to. Instead she clicked the receiver holder to make it sound as if she had hung up. She held her breath and listened to a conversation not intended for her ears.

Her aunt said, "Rand, I was having trouble sleeping tonight, and one of the nurses brought me one of those magazines—you know the trashy ones that leave ink all over your hands?"

"I know the ones you mean. And I think I know what was in it. A picture of me and Chelsea? It's not what you think."

"A picture of you and Chelsea?" Hetta asked, baffled. "No. It's something *about* Chelsea."

"The eating disorder clinic? She knows. Hetta, she seems quite good at coping with the unrelenting spotlight of the press."

Chelsea's sense of righteous indignation toward him wavered. Reading between the lines, he was telling her aunt that Chelsea was stronger than she'd been given credit for!

"It's not about an eating disorder clinic," Hetta snapped impatiently. "Do you think I'd be phoning in the middle of the night about that kind of nonsense? Don't let her see the paper, Rand. She would be deeply hurt by it. Other papers may pick up this story. It is going to be everywhere by tomorrow."

"I'll protect her," Rand said quietly.

Now was not the time to savor the fierce protectiveness in his voice! Now was the time to prove to them all that she was a grown-up! That she could handle whatever the news said about her, that she could handle someone sending her mean letters.

Chelsea King could handle herself!

Really, if there was ever going to be any hope for this *thing* that sizzled in the air between her and Rand to become something else, didn't she have to prove that she could be trusted with the details of her own life? What if Rand thought he had to look after her forever?

Forever.

That sneaky little word kept attaching itself to her relationship with Rand, even when she wanted to be angry with him. Even when she wanted to protect herself against the power of what she was feeling for him.

She put down the phone very, very quietly.

The car keys were on the kitchen table. With her heart in her throat, she picked them up. Trust. He had trusted her enough to leave the keys out, he had trusted her enough that he had reconnected the phone.

Had he? Or had those merely been oversights?

She suspected Rand did not do oversights. She reminded herself that she was turning over a new leaf. That she was thinking things all the way through, that she was no longer giving in to the impulses that had controlled her whole life. On the other hand, the windows of opportunity could be small and brief. She could think things through a little more thoroughly once she was in the car, by herself.

So, before she could talk herself out of it, Chelsea stepped over Benjamin and went out the door.

"Cameron, stop the car."

"No."

Sarah watched helplessly as they drew up to the entrance of her grandfather's Southampton estate. The attendant recognized Cameron, opened the gate and waved them through.

"I can't do it," she whispered. "Cameron, I'm so scared I think I'm going to puke."

She slid him a look. He was unmoved by her threat, and he drove calmly up the long driveway to the house. He shut off the car in front of the house, not at the back, not at the servants' entrance. Was he expecting her to go through that front door?

"Sarah, what are you so afraid of?"

The words spilled out of her. "I'm afraid he won't like me. I'm afraid he'll think I'm just here to take advantage of him. I'm afraid he'll reject me." She fell silent, and then whispered, "I'm afraid he'll think I'm not good enough."

Cameron looked at her long and hard, then sighed and got out of the car. He opened her door, and when she showed no sign of moving, he tugged her arm. She came out of the car and his arms wrapped around her, strong and good, something truer in his touch than any other single truth she had ever known. He took her chin gently in his fingertips and guided her gaze up to his eyes.

"You're looking at this all wrong, Sarah."

"I am?"

"It's not about taking from Jake. It's about the gift you are giving to him. Knowledge of the daughter he never knew, and the most wondrous evidence of her existence. You."

"I'm not a wonder! I'm not!" She looked around wildly. She could run—

But his voice stopped her. It was indignant.

"You, not a wonder? My God, Sarah, everyone who has

met you has always been taken with that *something* about you. A life force, an honesty, an authentic way of being."

"Honesty?" She heard the hysterical note in her own voice. "I stole from a man who trusted me!"

"Did you? Or did you try to hold on to a little piece of something that belonged to you all along? You're his granddaughter, Sarah. You belong here as surely as Brandy or Jessie or Chelsea. Now start acting like it."

The words had the effect of a slap. She became very calm. She could feel her spine strengthening and lengthening, her chin tilting up.

"I'm ready," she said. She walked right through the front door and made her way unerringly to Jacob King's office.

James, Jake's secretary, was sitting at his desk outside the door. When he saw her his mouth fell open and then snapped shut. His animosity had obviously done nothing but increase since their last unfortunate meeting, when he had caught her with Jake's silver candlesticks clutched in her sweaty hands.

So, maybe not *everyone* had been taken with her, she thought grimly.

"You have a lot of nerve coming here," he said.

She felt Cameron behind her, could feel that he was about to speak, but she held up her hand. This couldn't be about Cameron seeing who she was. Or about James not seeing who she was. It had to be about *believing*. She, Sarah Jane McKenzie, had to believe who she was.

"Tell Mr. King I'm here," she said, looking James straight in the eye, probably the first time she had ever done that. She saw James flinch from the utter calm and the absolute authority in her voice. She saw, out of the corner of her eye, Cameron cover his mouth with his hand, but not before she saw his smile of approval.

Without waiting for James to tell her it was okay, she opened the door and then closed it behind her. Jacob King was hunched behind his desk. She felt the familiar wave of heat in this office, because Jake had the fire going in the fireplace, though it was a warm day.

She felt a wave of shame. He looked very old and exceedingly fragile. Sarah's shame was not that she had stolen trinkets from him. But that she had stolen what he had the least of. She had stolen time. She had wasted precious moments she could have been with him.

"Sarah," he said, looking up at her. It was not the voice of a man greeting a thief, but the voice of a father welcoming home his prodigal child.

At the absolute forgiveness in his eyes, and in his voice, Sarah let the tears come, silent and tortured. Jake, even though it cost him great effort, got up from his chair and came around the desk to her. He took her elbow and guided her to the couch in front of the fireplace.

"Don't cry, child," he said tenderly. "Talk to me."

He handed her a tissue, and waited while Sarah tried to compose herself.

"My grandmother's name was Fiona McKenzie," she finally said, her voice a thread of broken emotion. "You might be more familiar with her maiden name."

Jake went very still. Sarah spoke into the stillness, about a long ago love, about a long ago heartbreak, about a long ago secret child born, a girl.

"A daughter?" Jake whispered. "Are you telling me I have another daughter, that I know nothing about?"

"Had," Sarah told him, sadly. "She was my mother.

She's gone. And Fiona's gone. What's left is this. I want you to have it."

She passed him the leather-bound diary, and he traced the old cursive embossed letters *My Diary* with tender fingers. Slowly he opened the cover. On the first page, yellow with age, Fiona had written her name in girlish hand writing.

After a very long time, Jake looked up. His eyes were shiny with tears. "This is not all that's left."

"I'm sorry. Yes, it is."

"You are left," he said, his voice suddenly strong. "You are left, Sarah."

She nodded through the tears that flowed down her cheeks.

"My granddaughter," he whispered, his strength spent. "You are my granddaughter."

"Yes."

His hand reached out and covered hers. "Why didn't you tell me, child?"

"Because I wrote you a letter, and you never answered. I thought you didn't believe me.. Or didn't want to know."

"A letter?" He frowned. "I never got a letter. Wait. Wait! I did get a letter. On the same day I received some upsetting news about my health. It must have been the one I burned. By accident. Before I even opened it."

He pinched the bridge of his nose with his bony fingers and his head dropped. His shoulders shook.

"I'm sorry," Sarah said. He was crying, and tears from this strong man were almost more than she could bear. "I've upset you."

He lifted his head and gave her a smile that showed

his strength was not lessened by those tears, not one iota. "Yes, you have," he said. "You've upset me. It feels as if this is both the saddest and happiest day of my life. A daughter I never knew. It feels as if my heart is breaking. But then, a gift, a granddaughter. A beautiful granddaughter that my heart recognized from the first moment it saw her. A granddaughter who can help me know my daughter."

She put her arms around his thin shoulders and hugged him. Their tears mingled together.

All her life, Sarah's heart had been in chains. The relationships she had known that should have provided a child with a safe harbor had been eroded by bitterness and poverty, by perceived betrayals, by illness, by anger. Where there should have been love there had been need.

Her grandfather's tears melted the chains that a lifetime of hardship had wound around her tender, young heart.

There was a knock at the door, which her grandfather ignored. James came anyway.

"Not now," Jake said with a wave of his hand.

James stared at them, at the tears, at their closeness on the couch. The hostility in his gaze changed to bewilderment. "But, sir—"

"Not now!" Jake said imperiously.

But Cameron came in behind James. "I'm sorry, sir, it's important. It's about Chelsea."

"About Chelsea?" Jake said. Sarah saw terror in his eyes. What was going on with Chelsea that would bring that look?

"Yes," Cameron said, "about Chelsea, but not what you're thinking. One of the maids just brought us this."

It was one of those celebrity rags, and on the front was the curious headline, When Is A Princess Not A King?

The phone rang. James answered it and passed it to Cameron. He spoke in a low tone for a few seconds, and when he turned back to them his face was unusually pale.

"Chelsea's disappeared."

Chapter Nine

Rand heard the faintest click on the phone line. The phone system in this part of the world was antiquated, but he felt a tingle along his spine. Had Chelsea been listening? Had she just hung up the phone?

"What did the article say?" he asked Hetta, straining to hear sounds from the kitchen, a cupboard door opening, footsteps. He heard nothing.

"It said that Jake is not Chelsea's father. The story claims that she was the love child of her mother and some ne'er-do-well actor. The same one that her mother died with."

"Don't rumors fly about this family all the time?" He thought he heard something downstairs.

"Not that can be backed up with DNA evidence. New-fangled things. Cause more grief than good half the time," Hetta said.

Now was not the time to argue the merits of DNA. "I'll do my best to see Chelsea doesn't see any papers," Rand said, and then his whole body froze and the hair on the back of his neck stood up. That had definitely been the sound of the screen door snapping shut.

He dropped the phone and ran to the front window, just in time to see Chelsea racing across the yard to the car, her hair leaving a shimmering luminous trail in the faint moonlight as it swept behind her.

He shoved open the window. "Hey!" he yelled.

Chelsea didn't even turn toward the sound of his voice, though it seemed to egg her on to greater speed. She reached the car, put her hand on the door handle and then looked back at him for the first time. If he was not mistaken, she stuck out her tongue.

Leaving the phone dangling he raced down the stairs and out into the yard. He was just in time to see the car reach the end of the driveway. She pulled out of the farm with great drama—a spray of gravel and spinning tires.

He said a word he reserved for terrible occasions, then turned and ran back into the house. He gave Hetta the briefest explanation possible from the kitchen phone and terminated the call. The upstairs phone was still off the hook, and he had to waste precious seconds going back up there. He was further slowed by having to look up numbers. He felt as if he wanted to be moving at the speed of light and instead he was moving as if under water.

Damn her. She could be in danger!

Luckily he had contacts close by—or close by as the helicopter flies. And luckily that car that Chelsea had just departed in was equipped with an antitheft GPS. He was going to be able to map every inch of her journey as soon as he got his hands on the right equipment.

When he caught up with her, that was the end of being a professional. Not that he'd been entirely professional so far, or he wouldn't be dealing with this badly unraveling situation right now.

No, this had been entirely preventable. Because Rand Peabody had actually noticed he'd left the car keys on the kitchen table after they'd cleared away the wreckage of a boisterous poker game: rumpled cards, one torn in two, the popcorn they'd been using for poker chips all over the place, the laughter still sweet in the air. In the afterglow of those moments with her, he'd noticed the keys and he'd hesitated, and then decided he would give her a message that he thought she needed to hear. He trusted her. He knew her to be a smart, capable woman who would make the right choices.

"Ha-ha," he told himself, as he considered the possibility she had *played* him to get precisely what she had wanted all along. Outta here.

He'd never, ever let his guard down so badly before. But then, he was not the same man he had been. Not just before Chelsea, but before Rafik.

When he'd lost Rafik, on that terrible, terrible night that Rand himself had been rescued, Rand figured it had killed everything in him that would ever want to care about another human being, that would ever want connection, that would ever want to trust. Or love. Instead his friendship with the young Arab had precisely the opposite effect on Rand's life. Because he had known that different place, Rand had, without ever putting it into words, *craved* an end to his loneliness.

It hadn't been a conscious craving. Conscious things could be weeded out and terminated before they became troublesome. So, he would have never consciously pursued a relationship that would have given him relief from the emptiness in his heart. But when that relationship had been presented to him, Rand simply had not been able to resist. His heart had been ripe for the picking. He had been attracted to Chelsea's warmth like a man who had crossed the frozen tundra to find a cabin with a fire burning within. He had been weak. An unacceptable character defect in his world.

After he completed his phone calls, he crossed the hall into her bedroom, looking for clues to where she had gone and why. It was a chaotic mess—clothes everywhere, her suitcase open on the floor, makeup scattered over the dresser and the windowsill. A bra, black, made of lace and silk and black magic hung over her bedpost.

"Strength," he ordered himself. No more distractions. None.

He noticed a manila folder on the bed. He recognized it as his file, taken from his briefcase. Who knew when? In his weakness, he had not even glanced inside that briefcase since his arrival here.

He glared at the folder.

So, all the time he'd been thinking he was building a relationship of trust with Chelsea King, she'd been doing crafty things behind his back. Wearing sexy black bras under her clothes, pawing through his briefcase. It underscored the rather ugly theory that she might have been planning this from the first moment. It made him wonder if he was kidding himself that he knew her at all.

Had she deliberately lulled him into thinking she trusted him and liked him, so she could get her own way?

He wanted to believe it, because it made him angry, and anger felt better than the helplessness of being stuck in this house while she tore up some highway heading to who knew where. But even as he wanted to believe it, to stay in the power of that anger, he could not.

It just wasn't possible. She was a terrible actress. He'd seen that from the first hand of poker. Her face was an open book. Every thought she had played itself out in the glory of her eyes.

He thought of her face that morning they'd climbed to the top of that mountain, he thought of how adorable she had looked with chocolate cake batter on the tip of her nose. He thought of her sticking her hands under those mean-spirited chickens with increasing bravery. She had been determined to stay here for her aunt's sake. There had been no pretense about that.

He thought of her eyes on his face, intent, as he had told her his every single secret. No one was that good at pretending. Absolutely no one, and she was not good at pretending at all.

So, he had to assume she had left on impulse, probably because she had overheard her aunt say there was a newspaper story that would upset her. But the fact that her disappearance was not premeditated did not make it any less dangerous. Who was out there?

At least one person who would harm Chelsea if he had the chance.

Rand looked again at the file open on her bed. The telephone call from her aunt, coupled with the discovery she was being stalked, had made her take matters into her own hands. He knew her well enough to know she would have been terribly insulted to find out about the stalker, and to find out no one had told her.

No. That *he* had not told her. Now it was her turn. She was showing him!

If he had it to do again, would he tell her? He doubted it. He had orders. He had made the choice not to tell her because it had been conditioned into him from his earliest memory, the choice that men had to make over and over again. Honor or love. He had grown up learning that man was always involved in an age-old battle between those two powerful forces. By not telling her had he chosen honor? Or had he really gone into denial after spending these few days with her, unable to believe any threat to her could be real, unable to believe anyone could want to harm her? He had, quite simply, been blinded by love.

Love.

That word kept popping into his thoughts with pesky regularity. Did he love Chelsea? Did he love her enough? Didn't a man dishonor himself when he chose not to listen to what his own heart, what his soul was telling him? Certainly that would be what Rafik would think.

Could a man honor himself by choosing love? Could honor and love coexist in the same world?

He heard, with that finely trained part of him that heard sounds before they were quite sounds, a helicopter coming.

He gathered a few of his things and went downstairs. He just had time to fill Benjamin's food and water dish and set it, with Benjamin's beloved mat, out on the front porch. Then the helicopter was there. Rand crouched low, running toward it, shades of his old life.

But he was so aware he was a brand-new man, and he did not know if he could ever be a part of that old life again. He was also aware that when he caught up with Chelsea, it was professionalism be damned. He was kissing the living daylights out of that girl!

Chelsea liked the look of helpless fury on Rand's face as she left him in the dust in her aunt's driveway. That would show him how it felt to have your life wrested out of your control. Lack of control was obviously something he needed to learn about.

She had been much too kind to him so far, letting him be the boss, letting him make the rules. Next time she saw him, she was kissing him and seeing just how he controlled that!

And the next time she saw him was probably only an hour away, since she decided to be merciful. She wouldn't leave him hanging very long—it would be mean to make him worry too much. She'd go to Farewell, find the paper her aunt was talking about and then go back to Rand.

And kiss him.

She congratulated herself on an absolutely delicious plan. Who said she wasn't good at planning? She wondered what his lips would taste like. She wondered how long he would resist her, before he gave in. She wondered if she should even go to Farewell. She could turn around and go back right now....

But no, she decided to savor the anticipation she was feeling. She had waited her whole life to kiss that man. She could wait a few more minutes.

She wondered if he would return her kiss out of fury,

or out of gratitude to see her, or if one would melt into the other.

Farewell, Chelsea soon discovered, was not exactly what one would call a mecca of late night activity. It was now nearly three in the morning, and nothing was open, not even the bar in the local hotel. Finally, on the very outskirts of town, heading the opposite direction from her aunt's farm she found an all-night service sation and an attached convenience store that called itself a "Quickie Mart." Her friends would have found the sign hysterical.

As she got out of her car she noticed a man huddled by a Dumpster, and wondered, sadly, if it was Brody from the soup kitchen.

She went into the store. The gossip rag section of the newspaper racks were covered with variations on a theme: When Is A Princess Not A King?; Fall From Royalty; Is The Fairy Tale Over?

She grabbed several of the papers and a coffee and went to the checkout. The clerk, thankfully, was the one person in the world with absolutely no interest in Chelsea King, though he eyed her fifty-dollar bill with suspicion.

She climbed into the car, took a scalding sip of the coffee, which was dreadful, and read the first headline. She scowled. If she was getting the gist of this, the paper was claiming she was not Jake King's daughter. Claiming a hair sample taken from her very own hairbrush had been checked for DNA and she was the love child of her mother and the man her mother had died with.

She'd been two years old when her mother died! Did that mean her mother's companion that evening had been more than a friend? That she'd been having an affair of long standing? Surely such a thing would have turned up before now!

Chelsea had read a lot of gossip about herself and her family. She viewed the article with skepticism. She was a King! She knew she was!

But then she folded the paper over and saw a picture of the man the paper was claiming was her father. She had always thought she looked like her mother, had thought, in fact, she was the spitting image of her mother. Until the moment she saw that picture.

It was a male version of herself. The man was extremely handsome, laughing, his hair an extraordinary shade of silver-blond, and his eyes…

She gasped when she saw his eyes.

So, she was not a King. Not a princess. Not who anybody, including herself, thought she was. She was a fraud. Wasn't that exactly how she had felt her entire life? Like a fraud? Like if people found out what she was really like—that she couldn't read very well, for instance—that she would no longer be liked and admired?

The strangest sensation came over her. The budding of her self-pity curled on the vine. What Chelsea King felt suddenly, inexplicably, maybe miraculously, was gratitude. Gratitude that this story had hit now after she'd had this wonderful time with Rand. After she'd been where she'd needed to be when her aunt had the heart attack. After she'd reached the conclusion that everything happened for a reason. Even a week ago this news splashed across the headlines would have shattered her.

But her world felt so different now. Rand knew everything about her, or thought he did, and he liked her anyway. Respected her. Trusted her.

She thought of his eyes. Maybe, she thought, he even loved her. What else could explain the look in those eyes? Tenderness and yearning, some secret in them he would not reveal?

There was a possibility Rand loved her, and she was going to sit here in a parking lot feeling sorry for herself? No, she wasn't. She had an ally in him, and she had just treated him very, very badly. She had behaved impulsively and immaturely and he was probably suffering worry needlessly because of her. She would take these articles back and she and Rand would go over them together.

First, though, she wanted to call her father.

Should she? It was very late at night. He probably had not seen this yet. She hated the thought of her father being distressed. Hated it, but she didn't want to wake him with such terrible news. Could it wait until morning?

She debated, and then started the car. A shadow caught her eye, at the back side door. She glanced over to where the man had been huddled by the Dumpster. The spot was now empty. She hit the automatic door locks, but it was too late. The back door of her vehicle opened and a man slid in.

She had done it again, she realized absurdly. She'd been ruled by impulse, not thought things through, not connected all the dots that needed connecting. She had just read about the stalker. And had she taken the extra precaution of locking her doors? No, she hadn't. Which was probably precisely why she had not been let in on the big secret to begin with.

What were chances that a stalker had tracked her to Farewell, and that their paths had collided at the all-night store? Slim to none, she thought with relief.

"Brody?" she asked tentatively. She glanced in the rearview mirror. Her heart hammered so hard in her chest she thought she would die before the man who had gotten into her back seat managed to kill her. He leaned forward, and shock rippled through her. It was not Brody. But it was someone she knew. It was Burton, from her apartment complex in California.

"Hello, Chelsea," he said with deep satisfaction.

Chelsea. That wasn't good. It had always been Miss King before.

"Burton," she said, forcing her tone to be light. "What a pleasant surprise! Was that you I saw the other day at Bounty Kitchen?"

"Didn't say hi then, did ya?"

"I didn't think it could really be you! I mean what are the chances we'd both end up at the same place in Farewell?"

Twice.

He was silent.

"What are you doing here?" she asked, trying to keep her tone chatty, breezy, *unafraid*. The poker lessons seemed to be helping.

"You know what I'm doing here."

"I do?" she asked innocently. "No, I really don't."

"I wrote those letters."

Now was the time to play dumb. She should be good at it. She'd been doing it her whole life.

"What letters?" she asked. "You've been writing me letters?"

She kept her eyes glued on the mirror, looking for her opportunity to jump out of the car. Her hand inched toward the door handle. Suddenly she felt something cold and hard pressed behind her ear. She knew, instinctively, it was a gun.

"I don't open my own mail," she said.

"That's too bad. Start the car and drive away. Don't do nothing foolish."

Well, she'd already done something foolish. She'd left Rand to come here by herself.

"Are you kidnapping me?" she asked, trying to keep him talking, trying to make him *connect* to her as a human being, not as whatever it was she had become in his mind.

"Something like that," he muttered.

"Because it won't do you a bit of good. Look at the paper."

Carefully she handed it to him. He only glanced at it. "I don't care about none of that."

"You don't care that I'm not really a King?"

"I'm not kidnapping you for the money, sweetheart."

Sweetheart. Even worse than Chelsea. Things were going downhill, and fast.

"Well, why then?" As if glancing through those horrible letters had not given her a pretty good idea. But she had to keep up the pretense that she didn't know about the letters, and that this was nothing serious, a case of running into an acquaintance unexpectedly.

"Does the fact that you aren't a real King make my chances any better?" he growled, and then answered himself, "No."

"Your chances at what?" she asked.

"See? Even if you're not a King, you would never

think of a guy like me in *that* way would you? I'd always just be the janitor. Invisible."

"I never thought of you as invisible," she assured him hastily. "In fact, I found the perfect gift to give your sister from me. It's a scarf that I wore to the Emmy awards. Real silk. Red. Vera Wang." She was making this up as she went along.

But apparently when it came to making things up, she was an amateur compared to her passenger.

"I don't have a sister," he said.

Part of her wanted to remind him, and churlishly at that, that he had asked her for a souvenir for his sister. Part of her wanted to survive enough that she didn't say anything.

"Drive," he said.

And she did, trying to think feverishly, but no ideas came. Nothing. Nothing. Nothing. And then: *If everything had a reason, what could be the reason for this?*

She was young, she had just discovered she was in love. This would be an absolutely inopportune time to die!

"Take that road," he said.

It looked dark and scary and like it twisted away from town up the dark mountain. It registered with her, really registered, that there was a very good possibility she was going to die.

She knew it was a measure of how far she'd come in the last few days that the pity she felt was not for herself. She thought of her father. The man she had thought of as her father for her whole life. She thought of him dealing with these two blows: finding out she was not really his, and then…

In her heart, she thought *I don't care what the papers say. I am Jake King's daughter. I am his heart and he is mine. If he did not give me life, he gave me spirit and spunk and all the things I have been discovering about myself in the last few days.*

Her father had sent her here, because he knew about those letters. He had wanted to protect her. Did he have another agenda? Had he known, all along, that she was short-changing herself? Had he known there would be something about that farm that would change her? She wished he could see her now. She wished her father could have seen her patting the pig.

Chelsea thought of Rand, and allowed herself to feel the sting of regret. She had not kissed him. She had not given in to the temptation of crossing the hall to his room. If she had done these things—followed her heart instead of the rules imposed by him—she wouldn't be here right now. Rand would come for her. But it would probably be too late.

Then the reason came to her. The message was so clear it might have been delivered by angels. If Rand was to rescue her from this situation it would set up the most terrible pattern: She did not want him to think of himself as her protector. She did not want to be his job. She wanted to be his soft place to fall, his equal, his playmate, his companion, his lover, his poker partner.

So, as ridiculous as it was, she was here alone for a reason. But that didn't mean she could not try to figure out what Rand would do if he was here. He would be analytical, alert, open to possibility. And he wouldn't take any crap from anybody!

She was all done being rescued by others for her own stupid choices. She was taking charge right here, right now. She was taking responsibility for herself.

"Hey! I told you to turn."

She wasn't going down that dark and creepy road with the equally dark and creepy man who had written those letters to her. She just wasn't. He could shoot her right now if he wanted to. Then it occurred to her he wasn't going to shoot her if she was driving—and the faster she was driving the less likely he would be to shoot her, because it would be putting his own precious hide in jeopardy.

She turned alright. She stepped on the gas, and when the car was shooting down the highway, she hit the brakes and spun that car around, back toward Farewell.

Burton, who had not put on his seat belt, rocked to one side of the car.

"I'm going to shoot you!"

"You go ahead!" She could see the lights of the convenience store and gas station. She stepped on the gas harder.

Her mind was calculating, figuring odds. She was wearing a seat belt, and he wasn't. That seemed to put the odds in her favor. She was a better poker player than she had been a week ago.

She aimed her car at a telephone pole.

She heard him shrieking at her to stop, but she didn't. She felt her nerve faltering, then she thought of Rand and pressed the gas farther. She heard a tremendous crack, felt, for an instant, the impact of hitting the pole, of going from sixty to zero in the blink of an eye, and then she knew no more.

Chapter Ten

Her head really, really hurt. She could hear voices, subdued, but they were voices she knew. Her sisters. She tried to pry open her eyes, but the effort hurt, and the slivers of light that penetrated the darkness felt shattering.

She heard another voice, deep and familiar. She thought *I am dreaming*. Or perhaps she was dead, because Rand did not know her sisters.

The thought that she might be dead gave her the impetus to try to open her eyes again, curious about what heaven would look like, thrilled that it contained people she loved. But did that mean they were all dead?

She opened her eyes and smiled weakly with relief. No, they were all alive, even her. The room was white and sterile, obviously a hospital room. There were flowers on every available surface.

Love, she thought groggily. *I am surrounded by love*.

She saw Brandy first and then Jessie and then...Rand.

She frowned. He hardly even looked like *her* Rand, the worry etched around his eyes, exhaustion in the slump of those big shoulders. They all looked exhausted and so, so worried.

"Hey," she said, wanting to reassure them. *I'm okay. Don't worry. Thank you for loving me.*

But the *hey* didn't come out strong at all, but as a mere croak, and she couldn't say the rest of it. Still, it was strong enough that they came to her bedside.

Brandy and Jessie were on one side of the bed, their hands wrapped around hers. And Rand was on the other. He took her hand, tenderly brushed hair from her face, then he dropped her hand abruptly.

"I'll go get the doctor." He was gone.

Brandy saw the look on her face. "Don't worry, he'll be right back."

But when the doctor came in, Rand was not with him, nor did he come back in after the doctor had left.

"That rat," Chelsea said.

Her sisters laughed, the laughter containing some of the pure giddiness of weariness and relief mixed. "The doctor?" Jessica asked.

"The doctor?" Chelsea shot back. "Rand!"

Jessie and Brandy both looked troubled. "Chelsea he's been up day and night. He hasn't left your bedside."

He loves me, Chelsea thought with satisfaction.

"He feels so guilty," Brandy said. "He thinks it's his fault."

"It's more than that," Chelsea informed her sisters.

"It is?"

"That man is scared to death."

They exchanged looks, as if she might be delirious. "He doesn't really have the look of someone who scares easily," Jessie said carefully.

"Harrumph. He knows I plan to kiss him until he's senseless as soon as he gets close enough," Chelsea declared.

"Kiss him?" Brandy said. "Oh dear, I don't think that's a very good idea."

"Why not?" Chelsea demanded.

Jessie leaned close and whispered, "Your lips are fatter than Mohammed after ten rounds with George."

Chelsea touched her lip and winced. She felt robbed! She was not going to be kissing anyone anytime soon.

"Do I look awful?" she whimpered.

Her sisters exchanged glances that let her know they planned to whitewash it.

She sighed. "I look awful." Then her energy was gone, and her sisters each kissed her cheek and left the room.

The next time she woke the room was dark and she was alone. But for some reason *I look awful* was stuck in her mind. Despite her aching head and a horrible nightgown she managed to get out of bed and head for the bathroom.

"Hey, get back in bed!"

She jumped. Rand was in the chair by the window. "I want to see what I look like. And I'm not taking orders from you!"

"Look what happened the last time you didn't take orders from me!"

"You didn't specifically tell me not to leave the house." She folded her arms over her chest.

"Get back in bed before you fall over, Chelsea. How's that for specific?"

Even though she felt woozy, she looked at him mutinously and stood her ground.

He was in front of her before she could blink. With exquisite tenderness that belied the stern expression on his face, he scooped her up, crossed the room, tucked her back in bed.

"I want to know what I look like!" she said, but not as strongly as before, woozy from standing, woozier from having had his arms around her so briefly.

"Remember that time I suggested blacking out your tooth as a disguise?"

She nodded.

"You look worse than that. Swollen mouth, no teeth, stitches and one black eye."

"No teeth?" She touched her mouth. All her teeth were there.

"See how much better you feel about the black eye and stitches now?" His tone was teasing but his eyes were not. His eyes were haunted.

"What happened to Burton?" she asked.

Rand told her Burton had gone right through the windshield. He had been flown to a trauma center and it looked like he would recover enough to stand trial for stalking, kidnapping and attempted murder.

Rand's expression got very dark as he talked about it. He said he'd been tracking the car from a helicopter using a very sophisticated GPS. If he'd just been a few minutes sooner, maybe she wouldn't have had to hit the pole, maybe… His voice faded away, but the haunted look in his eyes got worse.

"Rand, what's wrong?" she whispered.

"I failed," he said simply. "It was my job to make sure you didn't come to harm, and I failed."

She could see that he meant it, and she could see that handling this in a kindly way would be exactly the wrong thing to do. He needed a blast, and he needed it now! "Have I ever been really angry at you?" she demanded.

"Several times," he said dryly. "Remember the cell phone?"

That cell phone seemed like a long, long time ago!

"That was just a warm-up," she warned him. "You didn't fail me. How can you take responsibility for my actions?"

"It was my job," he said stubbornly, "to protect you."

"Rand, get real. No one on earth has ever been able to make me do anything I didn't want to do. It's not going to start with you, and you might as well get used to that right now."

He was glaring at her. "Get used to it?"

"That's right."

"Why would I want to get used to it? You're bossy and stubborn, and by your own admission, impossible to control."

"News bulletin—love is not about control."

"Who said anything about love?"

"Don't even think you can pretend you don't love me," she said, playing the most important hand of her life, laying every card she had right out there on the table. "That's why you better get used to it. Because you love me. Isn't that really what you're afraid of?"

His mouth moved but not a single sound came out.

"I think now would be a good time for you to kiss me," she said.

"Really? Like I said, bossy. For your information, it was always my plan to kiss you when I caught up with you. To kiss the living daylights out of you, as a matter of fact. But as always, nothing goes according to my plan with you."

"Why's that?"

"If I kissed you right now, you'd probably faint. Your lips look like collagen on steroids."

"Oh. Well, could you kiss me somewhere it doesn't hurt?" she asked him.

"You know what is so confusing about you? You look like an angel and act like a rottweiler."

"Admit you love me," she said.

He sighed.

"Because, Rand, I love you. I love you. You were my last thought before I hit that pole. You were my first thought when I awoke. You." Her last card. Had she played it well?

He surveyed her face solemnly, and then sat on the edge of the bed. He kissed the tip of her nose, her left cheekbone, the side of her ear.

"Do you want to know what I found out with that gun pressed behind my ear?" she whispered.

He lay his forehead against her shoulder, shuddered, nodded, ever so slightly.

"I think it's something you already knew: in a situation like that you find out who you really are. It's the crash course in self-actualization. So, I am not a spoiled brat. And I'm not a princess, either. I am not a dummy because I could never learn to read or write properly. What I am is a strong, resilient, *capable* woman. Worthy of you."

He reared back from her, took in her eyes and the set of her chin. She smiled, in spite of feeling incredibly tired. Her eyes closed again.

Did he say *I love you* or did she dream it? Did she fall asleep with his lips in her hair, or was that dream, too?

When she awoke next time, it was to the sound of laughter. A table had been set up at the end of her bed, by the window, and her sisters and Rand were playing cards.

"He cheats, " she warned them.

"I knew it," Jessica said. She reached across the table and relieved him of the watch that was sitting in front of him.

Chelsea regarded her sisters affectionately. The princesses. One brave. One brainy. One beautiful. Then she remembered what she had learned the night all this had happened.

"It's true, isn't it?" she said, watching them. "What the paper said that night?"

Rand excused himself, knowing this was a personal and very painful family matter. Brandy and Jessica sat on her bed. "We share the same mother," Jessie finally said. "We are sisters. Even if I didn't have a drop of the same blood as you, you would always be my sister. Do you understand?"

Chelsea nodded. "Is Daddy okay?"

"He's shaken. But all he wants to know is that you're happy." Brandy's eyes went to where Rand had just gone out the door. "And you're happy, aren't you, Chelsea?"

Her eyes, too, drifted to the door. She nodded.

Her sisters climbed into the narrow bed with her, one on each side, and they talked about their mother.

About how Jessie had suspected this since she was a teenager herself and carried the burden of knowing.

"I actually feel relieved that it's out," Jessie said.

They all agreed it was better to have no more secrets. And then they talked and remembered and laughed. Her sisters were happy, and so, so in love. Brandy told her about her life with Clint and Becky, Jessie talked about her honeymoon with Garner.

Chelsea fell asleep to stories of love, and she dreamed of green eyes and gorgeous lips and babies. The next morning she awoke to find Aunt Hetta in the room.

She was thrilled to see her aunt. "How are you? How are you feeling?"

"I think the question is how are you?"

"I'm fine. Happy to be alive."

Hetta laughed. "Me, too. They won't let me out yet, but at least we're in the same hospital. I've had lots of company. I've even started a little business to help me with my medical bills."

"What?"

"I'm selling autographed pictures of you."

"But I didn't autograph any pictures!"

"I just sign them myself," Hetta said with no remorse. "No one knows the difference. If they're foolish enough to spend their money on something like that, then they deserve what they get."

"You should sell some to the papers—that's where the big money is."

"Harrumph! I wouldn't sell a rotten potato to those scum. Not after the way they told that story about you."

"It's only a story," Chelsea said. "Granted, a true story, but it really doesn't change who I am."

"You're a different girl than the one who got out of the car a week ago," Hetta said, not without satisfaction.

"No, I don't think that's quite it. I think I'm just learning to let the real me out. So how is Benjamin? And the chickens? Who on earth is looking after everything?"

"Oh, Rand found me some nice young fella, Brody. I like him. I'm hoping he'll stay on as my farmhand once I'm outta here. Especially since I have a wedding to go to."

"A wedding?" Chelsea blinked.

"Oh!" Hetta looked distraught, as if she had said something she wasn't supposed to say.

"Funny, isn't it," Chelsea said after a while, "that you and I share a handicap, even though we aren't blood-related."

"Maybe it's more common than people think," Hetta said. "You're fixing to do something about that, I guess."

"How do you know?"

"Oh, dear, you've been mumbling away in your dreams."

"I have?" Chelsea could feel her cheeks burning. "Have I… er…mentioned any names?"

"Oh, yes, you have. Over and over and over."

A nurse came in just then and glared at Hetta. "Miss King, your whole floor is in an uproar looking for you." Hetta got up, looking quite pleased by that.

After she'd left, the nurse turned to Chelsea. "Did she get you to autograph some more pictures? I bought two from her for my grandchildren."

Chelsea said, deadpan, "Why, yes, she did."

Moments later her sisters came in. "We have a surprise for you," they announced. "Close your eyes."

Chelsea closed her eyes and heard the door whisper open. *Please be Rand. With a ring.* Her aunt *had* mentioned a wedding.

"Open your eyes," Jessie said gently.

Chelsea opened her eyes. Sarah Jane McKenzie stood beside her. Chelsea blinked. She had been so angry at Sarah, for stealing from her father, for taking off without a word to anyone. How could she have felt so angry, and yet be so happy to see her?

Sarah looked different. It wasn't the way she was dressed—the jeans still looked like they had come from the bargain bin at the thrift store. But, jeans aside, Sarah looked like a queen. There was no slump in those shoulders, nothing the least furtive or hang-dog about her expression. There was something very, very different in the way she carried herself and in the light that shone in her eyes.

Her sisters slipped out the door.

Sarah took her hand. "I have a long story to tell you," Sarah said. "I hope after you hear it you will forgive me. Do you feel up to it?"

Chelsea nodded, and Sarah sat down beside the bed but never let go of her hand. She talked about her hard childhood and her mother's death and the meanness of the man she thought was her grandfather. Then she talked about finding a diary and about what that diary said. By the time she was done, tears were rolling down her cheeks.

"Are you telling me you're my sister?" Chelsea said confused. The story wasn't making any sense. If her father had had an affair with—

"No," Sarah said. "My mother would have been your half sister."

"Oh my," Chelsea said. "Am I your aunt?"

Sarah nodded.

Chelsea squealed with delight and began to cry and laugh and cry some more. "Sarah, I can't believe this. I'm an aunt."

She sobered. "But of course, you aren't really my niece, because I'm not really Jake's daughter. You're related to my sisters but not to me."

Sarah squeezed her hand harder, and Chelsea saw that new thing in her eyes: confidence, a radiant belief in herself.

"How ironic," Chelsea said slowly and softly, "that you are really the princess, not me."

Sarah laughed. "Wasn't there a fairy tale that went something like this?"

"I think so."

"And I think the moral of that story was that you are what you think you are, Chelsea. What has always made you a princess is what is inside you. You were kind to me from the first moment you met me. That means so much more to me than if you had been kind to me after you knew I was related to you. The beauty of your soul and your spirit shines through. It never had a thing to do with the dresses or the parties or the people you hung out with."

"Well, maybe that little Michael Kors dress helped," Chelsea teased, and then she and Sarah laughed together, sisters of the heart.

Chelsea felt the simple and profound truth of what Sarah was saying because had she not always *known* exactly who Sarah was, even when the girl had lived in that awful motel and worn shabby clothes? Had Sarah's essence not shone through? That was why it had been such a shock to hear that Sarah had stolen from them and disappeared into the night. Because that was not who Sarah was.

What made people noble, truly noble, was not what they'd been given but how they handled *what* they'd been given, gifts and challenges.

"Chelsea, let me tell you something. You and I are family. I don't care if I'm not real blood."

"Aren't you something?" Chelsea said, smiling at Sarah's new confidence. "My God, you are just going to take this world by storm."

Sarah laughed, and then Chelsea noticed the ring and grabbed her finger. "You're engaged? Is that the wedding Hetta was talking about?"

Sarah blushed. "Cameron and I. When the time is right. When your health is good enough, when Grandpa feels up to it."

Chelsea, realized, shocked, *Grandpa* was her dad.

"Wow," she said. "Wow."

Rand sat at the edge of the bed and watched her sleep. He finally had her to himself, and he was glad. He loved watching her.

The headlines had finally died down. Chelsea King Nearly Killed By Stalker had pushed the other story, about her DNA, right out of the headlines. For that, Rand was glad. He had talked to her sisters. Jessie, in particular was dealing with tremendous guilt, because she had suspected all along.

But Rand saw simple truths when he was with Chelsea's sisters. They were strong, loving, beautiful women and they would help Chelsea cope with this. They would all come through it even better, stronger, more bonded than they had been before.

Rand had also seen headlines with pictures of him going in the hospital doors, coupled with the picture taken earlier of him holding Chelsea in the front seat of the car. Those headlines read The Princess And The Peabody as if they'd already forgotten that just last week they had been crowing Chelsea wasn't a princess at all.

Thankfully Rand's past was a sealed book. They had nothing on him. His presence in Chelsea's life was a mystery, and that's exactly how he wanted it to remain, until he sorted things out with her.

What was he going to sort out?

He hadn't even gotten his kiss yet, at least not how he wanted to kiss her, and he felt that moment was going to help him make a lot of decisions. He would never forget, for as long as he lived, the GPS leading him to the accident scene just moments after it happened. Seeing her crumpled over the steering wheel, so pale, the blood on her forehead making her look even paler. Knowing in that moment a truth it might have taken him a lot longer to realize to under different circumstances.

He loved her.

He was never leaving her.

He was not wasting any more time debating what was right and what was wrong. His heart knew the answer.

He'd called Jake and resigned as her bodyguard right then and there. So that when she woke up again, he could do what he most wanted to do. Be with her. Okay, and kiss her, though the fat lip had changed his plan.

She awoke then.

"Hi," she whispered.

"Hi."

She told him about her day, about Sarah.

"It's weird," she said. "She's really a King, and I'm really not."

He knew then the time had come. To find his answer. He leaned over the railing of the bed and kissed her on the lips.

"Does that hurt?" he asked softly.

"No." Her lips reached for his again, greedy.

He took them again and had his answer. For kissing her, was the most amazing experience in a life that had held many amazing experiences. In her kiss he tasted something wild and something innocent, something brilliant and something muted, something red-hot and something comfortingly warm. In her kiss he saw himself for the first time as a man worthy of being her hero, worthy of love.

In her kiss he sensed the future: mountains to climb, cakes to bake, laughter, poker games, children.

"You aren't going to be a King much longer, anyway," he told her, barely lifting his lips from hers.

"If that's a proposal it's a damn poor one," she said with mock indignation.

"How about we play a few hands of poker, winner takes all."

"No."

'What do you mean, no?"

"Rand, do it right!"

He chuckled. There she was with one black eye and her hair a mess and her lips puffy from injury and from being kissed, and she was still every inch a princess. He humored her. He got down on one knee by the side of her bed. Only then, gazing into the threaded mysteries of her eyes—*al-karrimataan*, the two precious things—he felt no humor. He felt the gravity of this moment.

She'd asked him, a long time ago, if prayers were answered. And he had wanted to say, no, they were not. Because he knew a man who had died too young who had prayed, every day, the simplest of prayers. On hopeless days, in a place as close to hell on earth as Rand had ever gotten, Rafik had prayed, with utter and simple confidence, for love to win. And was that not just what had happened?

In the end, Rand's friendship with that young man, a stranger from a strange land, had made him a man worthy of love, a man open to the mysteries, the power, the peace and the presence of love. Would Rafik have liked anything better than this? To see that his friend had not turned away from the lessons they had learned together, but that he had embraced them?

Rand was aware he had searched for this place, this moment in time, this woman for all his life. He had found what every man looks for: to be loved for everything that he was. He knew himself to be a complicated man: good and bad, deep and shallow, kind and judgmental, strong and weak. He saw that he had tried, all his life, to outrun his humanity by being perfect. It was only in his failure that he understood what a gift it was to be loved for exactly what he was.

"*Ma'ashuuqa,* beloved, the one I love passionately," Rand said. "Come with me for all the days of your life. Take my hand. Walk with me. Run with me. Build with me. Love with me. Pray with me."

The tears were flowing over the bruises on her face, and he caught them and held them to his lips. "*A'ashiiqa*—the one who loves passionately—will you come with me?"

She said, "I will."

Epilogue

It was Jacob Winston King's eighty-fourth birthday. He had not thought he would live to see this day, but his girls had showed extraordinary faith. They had known what gift he wanted and nothing was stopping them from giving it to him.

For weeks now, Kingsway had been abuzz with laughter and excitement, something so wonderful in the air that it filled him with the strength and hope that he needed to hang on for just a little while longer. He could not leave, not just yet. Though he dreamed now of Fiona and Simon almost every night. Waiting for him.

"Daddy, it's time."

His daughters, Brandgwen and Jessica stood in the doorway to his bedroom. He had always thought his daughters to be beautiful young women, but since their marriages what they had become transcended beauty.

He fought the clawing at his throat, as they each took an arm and helped him up. Jessica adjusted the white rose boutonniere on his jacket, Brandgwen fussed with his collar. And then, almost as if they had planned it, in unison they kissed him, one on each cheek. He felt their love for him. Better, he felt their love for their lives and their worlds. He sighed. His work here was nearly done.

They took him to the head of the curving staircase that led down to the main room of Kingsway. The room had been transformed: white silk draped from the ceilings; rows and rows of chairs faced the front windows; hundreds of crystal vases held lilies, pure white tipped with pink.

"Daddy, look."

He almost dared not to, but he turned as a hallway door opened.

His youngest daughter, his baby, Chelsea glided toward him, in a form-fitting white dress that left her slender shoulders bare and that swept the floor behind her. She had tiny red roses threaded through the silver of her hair.

She was not a baby anymore, and he could see the difference in her. She was a bride—a woman. She had begun to leave the child she had been behind her from the moment she had met Rand Peabody. Now, her transformation was complete. She looked serene and happy, not that there had been a bit of serenity in this house as she and her sisters had gone into overdrive to plan the wedding as a gift for him on his birthday.

"Daddy," she whispered, leaning toward him and kissing him on his cheek.

Not really his daughter? The papers had said it, and

science had proven it, but really the great mystery of who was family and who was not had not a thing to do with blood. Not a thing. It had everything to do with heaven.

His three girls, here together, gathered in joy. He felt as though his heart would burst with the simple love they poured over him.

Then another door in the hallway opened. They all turned and collectively gasped.

Sarah Jane McKenzie came out that door, but for a moment all he saw was her grandmother in the beauty of her features, in the light in her eyes, in the way she moved: graceful and self-confident in a white gown very different from Chelsea's, old-fashioned, high-collared, fastened at her throat with a cameo. Her dark, beautiful hair was threaded with white roses.

Fiona, his heart called silently, and from somewhere came the answer, whispered, *soon*.

"Sarah," he said out loud, and held out his hands to her.

Sarah took his hands, smiled into his eyes.

"You look beautiful," her aunts told her.

"Chelsea did something to the dress," Sarah muttered.

Jake hid a smile. Sarah had chosen her dress off a rack. She would never be completely able to leave her upbringing behind her. Chelsea, while pretending to completely respect the decision, had spirited the dress away and had the whole thing ripped apart and restyled by a friend who was a designer. He was glad she had. Sarah was a princess, and she deserved to look like one, especially today. If not for herself, then as part of this gift to him.

Brandy and Jessie released him, and the two beautiful brides looped their arms through his.

Once upon a time, Chelsea would never have shared this day with another. But she had delighted in the decision that she and her *niece* would marry the same day. They were more like sisters, the pair of them, forever squabbling and laughing, some connection between them that was unbelievable and unbreakable, though they were no more related by blood than he and Chelsea were.

The orchestra sounded the opening notes of the wedding march, and though it looked as though he were guiding his daughter and granddaughter down the steps, he was not. They were guiding him. Their love carried him as his own strength flagged.

He had a great sense, as he moved slowly down those stairs toward the men who waited, of the life force passing from one generation to the next. The men who waited down there were good men. Warriors.

Still, as Jake stood before the minister, finally, it took all that remained of his strength to say he gave away these women.

Yes, these were good, good men who had claimed the hearts of Sarah and Chelsea, but what would his children—his beloved girls—do without their father to look after them? He found his seat as the ceremony began, and pondered that. Truth came to him between the lines of that age-old ceremony. He had made a last wish for each of his daughters: for their happiness, for their love.

But really, he was not egotistical or foolish enough to believe the power of Jacob Winston King's will had been enough to bring about all the events that had transpired since he had made that wish. No, his wish had been heard by a compassionate universe, a power greater than himself had been hard at work. That power had brought him more than he had ever asked for. Not just happiness for his daughters, but two new grand-daughters, Clint and Brandy's baby daughter Becky, and Sarah, the legacy of a long ago love.

Jacob Winston King felt peace in the sudden and searing knowledge that yes, he would go, and he would go soon, but his daughters and their families and his granddaughters and all the grandchildren he would never meet would always be looked after.

For there was a power so great that all men were humbled in the face of it, a power so great it could heal wounds that were deep and crippling, a power so great it could go back in time and make all that had been wrong right, a power so great that in the face of any challenge a man could hear it whisper of hope. There was a name for this power. Its name was Love.

* * * * *

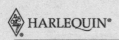

HARLEQUIN®

American ROMANCE®

IS PROUD TO PRESENT A
GUEST APPEARANCE BY

QUILL
BOOK
AWARD
WINNING
AUTHOR

NEW YORK TIMES bestselling author

DEBBIE MACOMBER

The Wyoming Kid

The story of an ex–rodeo cowboy,
a schoolteacher and their journey to the altar.

"Best-selling Macomber, with more than
100 romances and women's fiction titles
to her credit, sure has a way of pleasing readers."
—*Booklist* on *Between Friends*

**The Wyoming Kid is available from
Harlequin American Romance in July 2006.**

**Hidden in the secrets of antiquity,
lies the unimagined truth...**

Introducing

a brand-new line filled with mystery
and suspense, action and adventure,
and a fascinating look into history.

And it all begins with DESTINY.

In a sealed crypt in
France, where the
terrifying legend of
the beast of Gevaudan
begins to unravel,
Annja Creed discovers
a stunning artifact
that will seal her destiny.

*Available every other
month starting
July 2006, wherever
you buy books.*

GRA1

Page-turning drama...

Exotic, glamorous locations...

Intense emotion and passionate seduction...

Sheikhs, princes and billionaire tycoons...

This summer, may we suggest:

THE SHEIKH'S DISOBEDIENT BRIDE
by Jane Porter

On sale June.

AT THE GREEK TYCOON'S BIDDING
by Cathy Williams

On sale July.

THE ITALIAN MILLIONAIRE'S VIRGIN WIFE

On sale August.

With new titles to choose from every month,
discover a world of romance in our books written
by internationally bestselling authors.

HARLEQUIN *Presents*

It's the ultimate in quality romance!

Available wherever Harlequin books are sold.

www.eHarlequin.com   HPGEN06

If you enjoyed what you just read,
then we've got an offer you can't resist!

Take 2 bestselling love stories FREE!

Plus get a FREE surprise gift!

Four sisters.
A family legacy.
And someone is out to destroy it.

A captivating new limited continuity, launching June 2006

The most beautiful hotel in New Orleans,
and someone is out to destroy it. But mystery,
danger and some surprising family revelations
and discoveries won't stop the Marchand sisters
from protecting their birthright…
and finding love along the way.

If you enjoyed what you just read,
then we've got an offer you can't resist!

Take 2 bestselling
love stories FREE!

Plus get a FREE surprise gift!

Clip this page and mail it to Silhouette Reader Service™

IN U.S.A.	IN CANADA
3010 Walden Ave.	P.O. Box 609
P.O. Box 1867	Fort Erie, Ontario
Buffalo, N.Y. 14240-1867	L2A 5X3

YES! Please send me 2 free Silhouette Romance® novels and my free surprise gift. After receiving them, if I don't wish to receive anymore, I can return the shipping statement marked cancel. If I don't cancel, I will receive 4 brand-new novels every month, before they're available in stores! In the U.S.A., bill me at the bargain price of $3.57 plus 25¢ shipping and handling per book and applicable sales tax, if any*. In Canada, bill me at the bargain price of $4.05 plus 25¢ shipping and handling per book and applicable taxes**. That's the complete price and a savings of at least 10% off the cover prices—what a great deal! I understand that accepting the 2 free books and gift places me under no obligation ever to buy any books. I can always return a shipment and cancel at any time. Even if I never buy another book from Silhouette, the 2 free books and gift are mine to keep forever.

210 SDN DZ7L
310 SDN DZ7M

Name	(PLEASE PRINT)	
Address	Apt.#	
City	State/Prov.	Zip/Postal Code

Not valid to current Silhouette Romance® subscribers.

Want to try two free books from another series?
Call 1-800-873-8635 or visit www.morefreebooks.com.

* Terms and prices subject to change without notice. Sales tax applicable in N.Y.
** Canadian residents will be charged applicable provincial taxes and GST.
   All orders subject to approval. Offer limited to one per household.
   ® are registered trademarks owned and used by the trademark owner and or its licensee.

SROM04R   ©2004 Harlequin Enterprises Limited

SILHOUETTE *Romance*®

COMING NEXT MONTH

#1826 COMING HOME TO THE COWBOY—Patricia Thayer
The Brides of Bella Lucia
Rebecca Valentine might be thriving in the cutthroat world of
New York advertising, but she's losing the battle with her biological
clock. Then her latest assignment takes her to Mitchell Tucker's
ranch. With the cowboy's gentle nudging, Rebecca begins to see
a way to have it all....

#1827 WITH THIS KISS—Susan Meier
The Cupid Campaign
When Rayne Fegan's dad runs afoul of a loan shark and disappears,
she turns to the only man who can help her—her father's nemesis,
Officer Jericho Capriotti. But as their search brings them together,
will their family's feud stand in the way of her happiness?

#1828 NANNY AND THE BEAST—Donna Clayton
The Beast had defeated three of her firm's nannies when owner
Sophia Stanton stepped in to teach him a lesson. Sophia learns
quickly that when Michael Taylor shows fangs, he's really covering
deep wounds. And it isn't long before Sophia realizes that maybe she
is trying too hard to avoid a situation that could be a beauty
with this Beast....

#1829 THE HOMETOWN HERO RETURNS—
Julianna Morris
Luke McCade was gorgeous...*and* the last person Nicki Johansson
wanted to see. No longer the awkward girl from whom he could
steal kisses, Nicki had matured into a gorgeous woman. But could
Luke let go of the past to find a future with her?